I Shrunk my BF!

Book 1
OOOPs!

Katrina Kahler and John Zakour

D1464317

Table of Contents

Chapter 1

NO…you've gotta be kidding me! This is terrible! No, worse than terrible, it was like terrible multiplied to the max.

I stared down at my best friend Joe, as he looked helplessly back at me with his arms crossed. The frown on his face said:

OK Bella
How are you going to get me out of this?

The funny thing was, everything about him was exactly as it had been just a few seconds earlier. Except there was one HUGE difference. And this difference was seriously **major humongous.** You may think I'm exaggerating, but nope, I'm not. This was a big bad oops. It was also definitely not what either of us had been expecting.

First of all, Joe shouldn't even still be in the room. He should be back in medieval times watching knights in shining armor battle each other with cool swords and shields.

And I was supposed to be there with him. But I was more interested in seeing a real princess and a unicorn.

That had been our plan. But you know what they say, the best-laid plans can go astray. And to tell the truth, looking back at it now, this may not have been one of our better plans. As I stared down at my tiny, miniature friend, I could see we really should have thought this out a bit more.

"Oops, I guess this wasn't a time machine after all," I shouted to Joe.

"Yeah, kind of figured that out," Joe told me. "And no need to shout! I'm tiny, not deaf."

"Right," I said, looking down at him. I knew if we put our heads together we could find a way out of this.

We were so convinced that we could get my mom's time machine to work. We'd become obsessed with it, and had spent every spare afternoon and weekend working on it. Thinking back, maybe we were a bit too anxious. But you can't blame us! I mean who could resist the lure of traveling back in time?

We were sure this fancy machine was going to work just like the ones you see in the movies. Yeah sure, sometimes time travel in movies doesn't work out all *that* great but we were planning to be extra careful not to change any time lines. We were just going to watch history actually happening, not try to change it. After all, that's when all the bad stuff happens. We're two pretty smart kids. Just obviously not quite as smart as we thought. Still, this should really have worked out better!

We'd already done a test run on my sister's pet hamster.

We'd taken Honey, the hamster out of her cage and put her in front of the ray gun, and within seconds she had disappeared. We had no idea where she went, but 5 minutes later she was back and trying to get into her cage on the floor in front of us. She looked scared, and was desperate to get back inside her cage.

We thought the time machine worked! We just assumed that Honey was transported back in time. Maybe she was watching knights in shining armor or maybe a dinosaur or two, before being transported back here when the energy from the beam wore off.

We thought this was a time machine that Mom had started to build.

Mom's Time Machine

Why...because Mom always talked about how time travel would be so great for historians. They could observe the past as it really happened. People could see actual history. It all sounded so good. Then Mom stopped working on the project when she got busy with another two or three projects. I love my mom. She's got a great brain, she really is brilliant, but she does get easily distracted. So we decided to finish this one for her. After all Joe and I might not have three Ph.D.s and a medical degree like my mom, but we are still pretty sharp! Plus, we believe that when we put our minds together to do something, we can't be stopped!

Truthfully, we had already pictured the news headlines...

Yep! We were going to be super rich, even after giving my mom her fair share of the profits for starting this invention. We were going to be super famous, not only as great scientists but also as great adventurers through history! The world would love us.

We would have been able to quit school and have our own TV show. Just like those popular science shows on The Discovery channel, where they conduct experiments, blow things up, and do stuff they love.

Except this TV show would have our own unique spin to it. Plus, kids would love it, cause, well...we are kids.

As well, we had even come up with an awesome title...*Bella and Joe's Awesome Inventions in Coolness*.

We had it all planned. It would start simply with a trip back in time. Thinking back on our idea though, the fact that the machine didn't have a time or date dial on it, should have been a tip off to us. Yeah, it might have been better if we'd thought about that a bit. The problem was that we were anxious and blinded by science, okay more blinded by success and fame and fortune!

That's why today, just a few moments ago, we decided to put our time machine to the test. The real test, where Joe and I used ourselves as lab rats. Joe would go first. I'd fire the beam at him, he would disappear for a few minutes and then we'd reverse roles. We figured that the longer we kept the beam on somebody, the further back in time they would go.

We thought we'd start with a minor time change, like we did with the hamster, just a quick burst of energy from the time laser. Once we were sure that worked, we'd focus on going back further in time. The medieval time change was what we were looking forward to most of all.

Well, that was our plan! It just turned out not to be a very good plan. Really I should have realized it might not be a time machine...Mom would always babble on about, "Wouldn't it be great if we could shrink things! It would make storage and transportation of goods so much easier."

I really should have paid more attention to that. Mom had talked about working on a shrink ray. I just didn't realize that she'd started on it, and it was obvious that Joe and I had stumbled upon the shrink ray, NOT the time machine.

That would explain why Joe wasn't transported back in time at all. Instead, he stood in front of me, smaller than a toy. Funny thing is, at first I didn't realize this. As far as I could see he had disappeared, and all I had to do was wait 5 minutes for him to return. Just like my sister's hamster. After all that had been our plan. And I really hadn't planned on failure.

I'm a big believer in the power of positive thinking and so is my dad. He wrote this on my Bedroom wall...

BELLA

   If you believe hard enough you can make it happen! Do the work and get it done!

I read dad's sign and knew that I had achieved my goal, and Joe had been transported through time. Maybe to yesterday?

That was until I heard a sound coming from the direction of the floor, in the exact spot where Joe had just been standing only seconds earlier. At first I wasn't sure. I shook my head and rubbed my eyes, then I looked down. That's when I saw a little person in front of me, and that little person was my best friend, Joe.

"Joe, is that you?"

"Yep," he replied.

"So you didn't transport back in time to yesterday?"

"Nope! If I did I would have warned us not to do this stupid experiment."

"Joe, I'm not sure how to tell you, but I think this is a shrinking ray," I said.

"Yeah, I kind of figured that out," he replied. "At first I wondered if everything around me had increased in size."

"What a silly thing to think," I replied, smirking.

Joe raised his eyebrows and tilted his head to the side, "And you don't think SHRINKING ME was silly!"

I fought back a laugh. After all, when Joe shouted he sounded like an angry bee. But this wasn't the time to laugh. We had a little problem and we needed to fix it fast!

Chapter 2

Before I pick up from the present, I want to explain how we got here. Yeah, I know you know that I zapped Joe with a shrink ray that we thought was a time travel ray. Sure, it was not the best assumption to make, but I was desperate. I needed something cool to help my standing in school. When you're in middle school, what other kids think of you is very important. I know you're supposed to like yourself and be confident and all that. And I try, I really do. But it's a lot easier to be confident when people don't think of you as the laughing stock of your middle school. Let me tell you, middle school is hard enough without having people snicker when you walk by.

Of course, this all started with one of my mom's weirder inventions. Now don't get me wrong, I love my mom, she's super smart and she was a great athlete in college. She played shortstop for the national softball team. She's the total package of being smart, nice, dedicated and strong, plus my dad thinks she's really cute. The thing is, because my mom is so smart...she doesn't process information or ideas like other people. She sees advantages in things that most people don't. Which means sometimes she invents something that is really cool and revolutionary, only most people don't see that, especially when those people are middle school students.

The invention this time, and I'm not making this

up (though I wish I was), is a toilet that separates poop from wee and then clones the poop making more of it. Then the poop and the new poop is funneled through a high tech looking tube where mom mixes chemicals with it to make the poop even stronger.

Finally, the new improved poop is piped to our garden as super fertilizer. The good news is that this makes huge lush colorful veggies. The bad news is, this poop really STINKS. I can't begin to explain how bad it is…think of a wet skunk that just ate garlic and onions and is wrapped in stinky cheese. That smell you are imagining…isn't even close to the disgusting smell in our garden.

Mom insisted that this new fertilizer could help grow better healthier food all over the world. And it's the ultimate in recycling! It's as green as you can get. I told Mom that was fine but then I asked, "Well Mom, why can't you take out the terrible smell?"

Mom simply replied, "The smell is what gives it its kick. Sure we suffer a little, but sometimes science means suffering for the cause."

I begged Mom to take the stink out. I told her it would make the invention easier to get the people of the world to accept. She agreed to start working on it. I guess that's why she put her other inventions (like the one we thought was a time travel ray) on hold. That was some potentially good news. The bad news was that our house continued to smell. In fact, we became known as the PIG STY house. Mom and Dad thought it was a cute nickname. Of course they did, they didn't have to go to middle school.

Let's put it this way. Joe loves being at my house. It is practically his home away from home. But our place smelled so bad, not even Joe liked to come over...and when he did he usually brought a gas mask!

And of course, once the kids at school got a whiff of how bad our house smelled, my life became very difficult. Joe and my close friends would still talk to me because friends stick by you, even when your house reeks. But when you are in middle school you want as many people to like you as possible. That's kind of hard when kids refer to you as the *pig sty girl*.

To make matters even worse, Zac seemed to be avoiding me.

Yep, Zac the guy with big brown eyes and messy dark brown hair, would give me a polite but quick *hi* and then walk by. I really couldn't blame him. I had a hard enough time talking to him even under the best of circumstances. The first time he ever said anything to me was, "Hi Bella, how's it going?"

I responded, "Ah, ah, ah, good…I think." Yep that was my brilliant response to how's it going? I couldn't see my face at the time, but I knew I had to have turned a billion shades of bright red. I sounded so lame!

Zac said, "That's nice," then he slowly walked away.

But since my house had become the HOUSE OF POO and every kid at school knew about the smell, I didn't even get a *Hi* from Zac. After all who wants to be seen with a kid everybody calls *pigsty* girl. Even if I didn't smell like poo, which Joe insisted I didn't, my house certainly did. I love my mom. She's a smart and amazing person. But she has no idea what it's like to be a kid. After all, she must be almost 40! I doubt she can even remember back in the old days when she was my age. I'm betting kids were easier to please then, anyhow. There was no social media back in those days. I'm not even sure they had cable TV!

So I made my argument to my mom. I explained that while her amazing invention might be great for the world, it was really wrecking my social life. I whined and complained for days on end, until finally she promised to modify her procedure and find a way to take out the terrible smell.

In the end, she removed the poop-cloning device and transport system from our toilet. She stored it in her high tech lab, or as we liked to call it, the basement. I breathed a sigh of relief. For the first time in a long time, the place didn't smell of poop. With the smell gone, Joe started coming over more often, and he was leaving his gas mask at home!

***

That brings me pretty close to the situation at hand. During Joe's first trip to my house after a fairly lengthy week long absence, he was dying to check out the basement lab. I wanted to explore it with my best buddy also. We hoped we would find something truly amazing! I needed a big win to get back in the good graces of the kids at school. I needed something to make Zac notice me.

We had been down in the basement like a billion zillion times (okay maybe more like 40) and every time we would discover something new. This fateful day we found something super cool. It was a long laser beam like contraption. I remembered my mom mentioned that years and years ago, she tried to invent a time ray but could never get it to work. So she decided to shelve it in the basement until she had time to make the necessary adjustments. Then of course she got distracted by one of her many other projects. Somehow when she packed away the poop cloner, she must have pulled out the laser beam and left it sitting in full view. And that was how we happened to notice it.

"This has to be Mom's time ray machine!" I told Joe.

"Wow!" Joe exclaimed. "So cool! Why didn't she ever use it?"

"I guess she never got it to work…then, well…she got distracted."

"Maybe we can make it work!" Joe said.

"Joe, that's the best idea you've ever come up with!" I stared at him wide-eyed, my mind spinning with excitement. "Yes, let's do this! Let's perfect this time ray!"

I don't know why I thought this. I have no idea why two kids in middle school thought they could fix a time ray that a brilliant scientist with an M.D. and a bunch of Ph.D.s could not make work. I guess I was blinded by wanting to impress Zac and regain my mediocre reputation at school.

Joe and I spent the next week tinkering on the machine. Mom always took her main project upstairs so she could work on the kitchen table. She thought the light was better there, plus she liked being around the family. That meant Joe and I could tinker in private in the basement. Once Mom got rolling on one project she became 100% absorbed. So she didn't even realize that we were occupied downstairs.

After a few days, Joe and I tested the machine on my sister's hamster. That seemed to work. So we moved to the next stage, our live human test. That brings me back to the present....where I am standing foot to face with my best friend.

Chapter 3

Truthfully, at first I almost stepped on Joe. Now that would have been terrible…squishing my BFF – not to mention messy. Luckily I heard him (or something squeaking) from below. Grabbing a magnifying glass from the bench top, I leaned down to get a closer look. Standing with arms crossed and frowning was Joe.

"Thanks for not stomping on me!" he shouted, though I could barely hear him. To be honest, if I hadn't known he was talking, I would have taken his words as simple background noise.

"Joe, is that really you?" I asked, for lack of anything better to say.

"Well, duh…" he replied.

"Is this some sort of side effect from time travel?" I asked desperately.

Joe just shook his head. "No time travel. Well technically, I guess we have all traveled to the future from where we started this process, but nope, no out of the ordinary time travel."

"Don't worry buddy, I can fix this!" I told him.

"How?" he shouted.

I stood up and headed towards the ray gun. "I'll just reverse the beam. This must be my mom's shrinking device," I said.

"Ya think…" Joe was sounding slightly annoyed and sarcastic.

"Yes I know it is. I'm sure there is a reverse switch on it. I'll just flip the switch, then aim it at you and all

17

will be well," I stuttered.

"You know, Bella, I trust you. But somehow I get the feeling it's not going to be that easy."

I positioned myself behind the shrink ray machine. I had noticed a switch right beside the trigger. The switch moved forward and backward. It had been jammed earlier, but Joe and I oiled it to make it work better. I had assumed this would be a time reverse switch to help people move into the future...maybe. Or maybe bring them back from the past. Truthfully, I was too excited by the thoughts of stardom to really think that much.

I hit the switch. I fired the beam. Suddenly I felt a crackle of energy. Looking across the room I saw Joe standing there tapping his foot. He walked towards me. We were the same size. "It worked! It worked!!" I shouted.

Joe pointed up.

Looking up, I saw a giant shrink ray machine.

"Oh," I said. "Apparently I've shrunk myself now, too."

"Very good, Einstein," Joe said, arms crossed, eyebrows raised.

"Okay, we've been in worse situations!" I said, trying as hard as I could to sound like I believed it.

Joe continued to tap his foot. "When have we been in a worse situation?" he shouted. "We're toy size! We're bite size! We're like way small!"

"Well there was that time we forgot to study for Ms. Sandy's English test," I offered.

Joe shook his head. "Nope! Not even close."

I pointed at him. "The time we played a prank on that big bully, Bart Jackson, by gluing his locker shut?"

Joe shook his head. "He never found out it was us, so nope."

"How about the time that junk yard dog chased us when we were looking for spare parts?" I asked.

Joe shook his head. "Remember that dog was so old he didn't have any teeth. His bark really was worse than his bite. His breath was pretty bad too. But still not as bad as us BEING LIKE TWO INCHES TALL!

"Okay, Joe, I gotta admit, you MAY have a point. Shrinking ourselves is the worst thing that has ever happened to us... The good news is we've made science history, just not in the way that we'd planned."

Joe shook his head. "Not too sure that we want to be known as the stupid kids who shrunk themselves."

I gave him a half smile. "Well, the good news is that things can't get any worse! Right?"

Joe groaned. "Wrong again my friend."

"Wait, Joe how can it get worse than this?" I asked.

Joe pointed behind me. "A big nasty spider just dropped down on the floor and it looked hungry."

"You're joking, right, Joe?"

He groaned. "I so wish I was."

I turned, and there coming towards us was the biggest hairiest gray spider I had ever seen. I probably would have been a bit scared of this spider if I had been normal size. Now that I was smaller than spider size, I finally had to admit Joe was right, this was not our finest moment.

The spider stood there looking at us. I guessed he or she had no idea what to make of us. I don't know how well spiders can see or smell, but I could tell this spider knew we were something new.

I turned to Joe. "Look, we're perfectly fine."

"We're like two inches tall!" Joe shouted. "That's not fine!"

I shook my head in agreement. "That is true." I pointed to the spider. "But here's the thing, spiders only eat insects and we, my friend, are not insects."

"I know that. You know that. But the big question is...does the spider know that?"

"Look Joe, spiders aren't stupid. They know they don't eat people."

Joe stood there taking in my words. He scratched his head. "I'll give you that. But does Mr. Spider know we are people since, WE ARE TWO INCHES TALL!"

I stopped myself from rolling my eyes. "I get it Joe, you're upset. But trust me this will all work out, and then we'll have a cool wonderful story to tell."

"As long as we don't get eaten by a spider in your basement," Joe gulped, taking a step backwards.

"Joe, like I said, that's not going to happen…"

Joe shivered and pointed to the spider. "You better tell Mr. Spider that!"

I turned. Sure enough the spider was creeping towards us.

I jumped up and down, waving my arms. "Yo! Nasty looking spider, back off!" I shouted.

"Bella, you probably shouldn't call the spider nasty looking," Joe told me. "Let's not make it angry!"

"Joe! I'm pretty certain it doesn't speak English!" I said. "Plus, I'm just making noise and moving around to show this spider we aren't insects."

"Think about it Bella, how would an insect behave in front of a spider? Wouldn't it be making a bunch of noise and moving around panicking?"

I swallowed. Yep, that might have been a good point. Of course I couldn't admit that right now. "So Joe what do expect me to do? Quote Shakespeare to the spider? Tell him the Laws of Physics? Do some math tables?"

Joe took a few steps backward. "Whatever you're going to do, do it fast!" He retreated some more. My hero.

I turned to see the spider now lording over us. I could smell his breath. I thought his breath smelled like dead insects but that could have been my imagination. But his breath was the least of my problems right now.

Time to use my scientist brain to get me out of this. My scientist brain got me into this, I knew it could get me out too. Okay, maybe not the best logic, but believe me, it's hard to be logical when you are face to face with a big hairy spider. I figured Joe might have had a point. No way this spider couldn't be sure we weren't some new kind of tasty insect for it to chomp on. I did the only logical thing. I decided to convince this spider that there would be easier meals around this basement, than my friend and me.

I socked the spider right in the face. Normally I don't like to turn to violence, but in this case I thought it was the best way to go. I knew I couldn't really hurt the spider. I just wanted to give him or her something to think about. I thought for sure no flies or mosquitos would ever punch this spider in the face.

The spider took a step back. Then another and another. I stomped my foot at it. It turned and then scurried away. Joe walked up to me and patted me on the back. "Great job, Isabella!" he said.

I turned to him and rolled my eyes. "Thanks for backing me up there!" I made a point of letting him hear the sarcasm in my voice.

He lowered his eyes. "Yeah, sorry. Not my finest moment. But you know I've always had a thing about spiders! Even when I'm way bigger than them, they still freak me out. But you're right I should have stuck by your side."

I had forgotten about Joe's spider thing. I guess I wasn't as good a friend as I could have been.

I put a hand on Joe's shoulder. "That's okay buddy, we all have things we're scared of. I'm sure that spider learned his lesson and won't be bothering us anymore."'"

"Thanks for saving us, Isabella," he replied. "So what's the plan now?"

Chapter 4

I stood there studying our situation and taking in what was happening.

"I repeat, what's the plan?" Joe asked me, this time with a little nudge.

"I'm thinking," I told him.

"Sorry, I had no way of knowing that. It's not like you've got a light bulb over your head like in the comics!"

I thought about our early trial. We shot the hamster with the ray. He disappeared and then came back a few moments later. We assumed he had traveled into the past, but he actually must have shrunk down to a tiny size and then grown back. That was it.

"We just wait!" I told Joe.

"For what? A hungry bird to come by and snack on us?"

"Joe, there aren't any birds in our basement."

"Okay, how about a hungry rat? Can you tell me your basement doesn't have rats or mice?" Joe asked. "We're so small, even mice would think we looked like a nice meal."

My mom had always said she wanted to build a better mousetrap, but she'd never got around to it. So nope, I couldn't guarantee that our basement was mouse and rat free. "Joe we're going to be fine!" I promised, trying to sound confident.

"And you come to this conclusion, how?" he asked.

I pointed to Honey in her cage, on the floor in the corner of the room.

Joe shrugged. "So, we still have your sister's pet hamster...which is now larger than we are!"

"Joe, do the math!" I said.

Joe shook his head. "This is no time to be worried about homework!"

I held up a hand. "Think about Honey's history."

"We're still talking about the hamster, right?"

"Yes, Joe. Think about Honey the hamster!" I shouted.

Joe pointed. "She's right there in her cage. She looks happy enough."

I groaned. "Now think about our history with experimenting on Honey, the hamster..."

"We thought we sent her to the past. But then she came back." Joe said slowly.

"Almost there, Joe, almost there!"

He scratched his head. "But we didn't really send her back in time, we just shrank her."

"And?" I asked. Joe almost had this.

"She came back to normal size!" Joe said, jumping up and down.

"Ding ding ding!" I said. "Give the man a prize!"

"So all we need to do is wait and we too will grow back!" Joe concluded.

"Yep!" I said with far more confidence than I should have.

We made ourselves comfortable and sat down. We pulled out our phones. We figured we could check our Facebook and Instagram pages. That turned out to be a no go. For some reason (probably a good reason) our mini-phones couldn't pick up a Wi-Fi signal. And it looked like the shrinking process had drained the batteries anyway. That forced Joe and I to spend time the old fashion way...actually talking to each other.

"I'm thinking of a number between 1 and 1000!" Joe told me.

"500," I said half-heartedly.

"Wow you got it!" Joe told me. "Your turn to guess a number!"

Okay, not my ideal way to spend some time but I'd give it a try. "I'm thinking of a number between 1 and 10."

Joe raised his eyes. "Oh come on, that's too easy! I'll get this in like three guesses!"

"Then try!"

"Five!"

"Too High, Joe!"

"One!"

"Too low!"

"Three!"

"Bummer, too high Joe!"

He pointed at me. "Ha got it! It must be two!"

I shook my head no.

"Wait it has to be two! That's the only number between one and three...."

"Actually my number was two and a half!" I told him. Yeah, it might not have been playing fair, but the rules didn't say we couldn't use fractions.

Joe laughed. "Good one, Bella!"

That's why Joe, despite his flaws, was a great friend. He was very understanding of my ways. He never minded that I often wrote my own rules. He always stood by my side, or at least near my side.

We played twenty rounds of rock paper scissors. We played another twenty rounds of twenty questions. We did some finger fighting. I won three out of five matches. Joe suggested we have a contest to see who could fart the loudest. I told him no way, I'm a girl, I don't fart. But if I did, mine would certainly be the loudest. After killing as much time as we could, it started to become clear that maybe, just maybe, we wouldn't be turning back to normal size. I concluded we must have hit ourselves with way more of the beam than we had hit Honey with.

Joe brought it up first. "Ah, Bella, I hate to point this out but I don't think we're the right size yet," he said cautiously. He looked at all the giant objects around us. "I guess it's possible we grew back and everything else grew larger, but that would be another problem."

I forced myself to grin. "Yep, it looks like we need to be proactive," I said. "Now, what's the most scientific way to go about this?" I pondered.

"We could yell and scream really loudly and hope your mom hears us?" Joe offered.

"Ah Joe, how is that scientific?"

Joe rolled his eyes. "Duh! Your mom is a scientist. She's like really smart. Like smarter than a science and math teacher combined. I know she could figure out a way to make us big again!"

Joe had a good point. Mom was quite the brilliant scientist. The problem with getting Mom to help, was that I'd have to admit that I did something stupid. And I'm not keen on admitting that I did something stupid. Actually, I don't think of it as stupid. I think of it as being inventive.

But Mom being older than me, and not as open-minded as I am, might consider my idea not the smartest thing in the world to attempt. Especially using her machine on myself and my friend, when I had no idea what it could do to us. My mom could be so close-minded at times. I mean come on, she's a scientist. She should understand how brave we were…going where no man, woman or kid has ever gone before.

Joe looked at me. "You have your *I'm thinking* face on…" He stared at my thinking face. "I know you probably don't want to admit to your mom that you played with one of her inventions without telling her." He scratched his head, "After all you most likely don't want her to feel guilty about leaving this machine around so we could find it…"

I nodded. "Yes, very good point Joe." Yep he knew me well, almost too well.

"But," Joe said slowly. "I really don't see another way out of this. After all, your mom is a mom first, and a scientist second. I think she would see how she might have made a tiny mistake leaving the machine out in the open for us. I bet she'd be glad to help us out. It would help her right a wrong. Scientists love helping people. Right?"

Joe always rambled on and on when he got nervous. I guess I couldn't blame him for being anxious. After all, we were only slightly bigger than an insect. Looked like it was time to admit to our mistake and yell for help. I looked at Joe. I smiled. "You're right."

Joe took a step back. "I am?" He put his hand over his heart. "Say what? I'm not sure I've ever heard you say that!" He smiled widely. "Wow, I've never been so happy!"

I pointed to him. "You do understand we are bite sized now. Right? Not exactly a time to celebrate."

Joe kept smiling. "I don't mind being small and RIGHT!"

"MOM!" I yelled.

"MOMM!!!!"

"MOMMY!!"

"MOTHER!!!!"

I yelled louder and louder.

We looked up the basement stairs at the door. Nothing. I nudged Joe.

We both jumped up and down yelling:

"MOM!"

"BELLA's MOM!"

"MOM!"

"BELLA's SCIENTIST MOM!"

"MOTHER!"

"SUPER SMART LADY!" Joe yelled, waving his arms up and down.

I stopped yelling and looked at him. "Why the heck are you waving your arms?" I asked. "It's not like we're trying to signal a ship."

Joe shrugged. "I just felt like waving. I thought maybe it could push the sound waves farther."

I rolled my eyes. "That makes no sense!"

We heard the door above us open. Joe looked up and grinned. "See! I knew it would work!"

We heard a voice. "Bella? Bella? Do you have my darling little hamster? Bella? Where are you? You'd better not be running one of your crazy silly experiments on Honey! Bella! Answer me!" That voice belonged to my little sister Becky.

We heard Becky pounding down the wooden steps that led to the basement. Each step echoed through the room, shaking Joe and I. Man, we were small.

Of course Becky talked all the way down the stairs. "Bella? Bella? Where are you? Honey! Honey! Can you hear me, my sweet little hamster?"

"She does understand that her hamster can't talk, right?" Joe said. "Seriously though, that hamster can't talk, can it?" Joe asked me.

"No, of course not!" I snapped.

"Hey!" Joe snapped back. "In this house you never know. If your mom can invent a shrink ray then maybe she can make animals talk. I mean when you think about it, making animals talk makes more sense than shrinking people."

I put my hands on my hips. "Why does that make more sense? I mean what good could talking animals really be? But shrinking things would make transport and storage of things way easier," I pointed out.

Joe scratched his head. He grinned. "Man, Bella, that's right. You're so smart!"

If I was really smart, my best friend and I wouldn't be so small right now. Of course I wasn't going to bring that up at the moment. I needed Joe to trust me and have confidence in me. Somehow his confidence made *me* more confident.

I came up with what seemed like an easy decision. But trust me, nothing is easy when you're not even two inches tall.

"Joe, this may not be Mom, but Becky can still help us!" I said.

"You know she's not a scientist. Right?" Joe stated the obvious.

"Yes Joe, but Becky can bring us to a scientist!" I told him.

He stood for a moment, squinting. His eyes popped open. "Oh I get it!" Joe said.

Chapter 5

Becky stopped half way down the stairs. She peered into the basement and called:

"Honey, my honey, where are you?"

"Did my stinky sister leave you down here alone?"

"If that sister of mine hurt you, I will let her have it! Yeah, I know she's bigger than I am, but I am tricky and tough!"

"Plus I'm smarter....and I smell better."

Joe nudged me. "Wow, she really doesn't like you much."

"We have our issues, but she looks up to me!" I insisted.

"Why isn't she coming all the way down?" Joe asked.

I let out a breath. "She doesn't like the basement. It takes her a while to work up the courage."

"She's a smart girl," Joe said. "There is some pretty strange stuff down here."

"It's not that bad!"

Joe took a step back. He pointed at me. "OMG Bella! We're two inches tall!"

"But that was all our fault for thinking we're scientists!" I breathed in. "This isn't the time to argue. We need to figure out how to get out of here. And up there!" I pointed towards the stairs.

Walking towards the staircase that loomed in front of us, I looked up. I could hear Becky on the top step, still trying to work up the courage to come down. And of course still saying bad things about me.

"Bella, if you're down there and not talking to me, you're being extra stinky!"

"Bella, if you're trying to scare me, then you're being extra mean!"

"I'm not scared, Bella I'm just being careful."

"I'll be down there in a minute or two!"

Blocking Becky out of my mind for a moment, I looked up at the bottom stair. "Come over here!" I called to Joe.

Joe ran over to me. "What's the plan? Are we going to yell up to Becky?"

I shook my head. "I don't think that will work. But I bet we can climb these stairs and get closer!"

Joe stood at the base of the stair and cranked his neck upwards. He saw the stair had to be twice our height. "I think we have a better chance if we yell out to her."

I pointed up. "Give it a try!"

For the next couple of minutes, I listened to a two-inch Joe trying to jump and yell loud enough to get my crazed little sister to listen.

"Hey Becky, can you hear me?"

"Bella, Bella, Bella, why won't you answer me?"

"Becky! Becky! Listen!"

"Bella, why are you so mean?"

"Becky, stop talking for a minute and listen!!!"

"Mom, Bella is being mean to me!!!"

This went on until Joe finally figured out that Becky couldn't hear him, especially with her shouting down the stairs at the top of her lungs. He turned to me, "Okay let's try your plan."

"Great!" I said. Now I only needed to actually

come up with a plan. This couldn't be that hard. The stair had to be like seven inches high. I just needed to put Joe up on my shoulders. He could reach up and grab the stair above us. He could then pull himself up and then pull me up. We'd just repeat the process twenty times.

"Okay Joe, I'll boost you up onto my shoulders. You grab the stair above us and pull yourself up! Then you pull me up! This will be easy!"

Joe took in the size of the stair in front of him. Then he stared at me, not completely convinced. When no other option came to mind, he shrugged. "Worth a try!"

I bent down as low as I could. Luckily all those dance classes Dad insisted I take, had made my legs strong and flexible. Joe carefully stepped over me. He positioned each one of his legs over my shoulders. "Okay up!" he said.

Holding onto his legs, I pushed myself up straight. From on top of me, Joe extended his arms reaching for the stair top. "Darn, I can't quite grab it!" he said.

I moved a step or two closer. I pushed myself up high on my tiptoes. Joe reached up. I felt some of the weight leave my shoulders and back. But he still couldn't quite pull himself up.

"Almost got it!" he said, stretching out.

I stretched as far upwards as my body would allow me to.

Joe let out a fart. PPPPPPFRRRRRTTTT!

"Oh gross, Joe!" I shouted as loud as I could, while trying to hold my breath.

"Sorry, but that's what I needed!" he yelled. He pulled himself up onto the stair above.

I waved away the disgusting smell of Joe's fart. I

raised my arms in victory!

"We did it!" I shouted.

Joe lay down on the stair above and lowered his hand to me. "We sure did!" he replied, almost glowing with pride. "I think the fart propelled me!"

"Just pull me up!" I said.

I reached up. Joe took my arm. He pulled. I felt the pull. It had enough force to get me to stand on my tiptoes. Not nearly enough to pull me up the stair.

"Joe, use both hands!" I suggested firmly.

"Right! I got this!" Joe said. He leaned over and reached down with both his hands. I let him grab my arms. "Pull!" I shouted.

Joe pulled. I felt more force this time. Maybe, just maybe we could do this! We were just like those acrobats you see on TV. But then I felt all the force disappear. In fact, all the pulling on my arms turned to pushing. Joe rolled off the stair and landed on top of me.

Nope, we weren't anything like those acrobats you see on TV, we were more like the clowns.

"I think we're going to need another plan," I said.

"I so agree," Joe said from on top of me.

"Let's start with you getting off me!" I shouted.

"Right, good start!" Joe agreed.

Chapter 6

Joe stood up and dusted himself off. Neither of us seemed to be injured from his falling off the stair and onto me.

"Well at least we accomplished something," Joe told me.

"Which was?"

He grinned. "We learned we aren't good climbers."

Yeah, now it was obvious that we needed another way to get to the top. "We need to be carried up the stairs," I said very forcefully, like I had just made a great deduction.

Joe jumped up and down. "I got it! I got it! We just need to get Becky to carry us up."

It made sense. We really should have tried that first.

Becky continued to yell down the stairs:

"Bella! Bella, you'd better not be trying to scare me!"

"Bella, Bella, Bella! I know you must be down there; the lights are on!"

"Bella, did you forget to turn the lights off? Dad will be mad! Oh good, I can get you into trouble!"

Joe turned to me. "Boy, she really doesn't trust you."

I grinned weakly. "Yeah, I played a joke on her once. It wasn't a big deal. I hid behind an old box and jumped out at her when she came down here. Scared her so much that she wet her pants! At the time I couldn't stop laughing. It was hilarious!" I paused. "I guess she still has issues about that."

Joe shook his head at me. "I can understand that."

"Look Joe, I was a kid then. It was like last year. I feel bad about it," I admitted with a sigh. "I actually felt bad about it after it happened, so I took her for ice cream."

"Now that was nice!" Joe said.

"Yeah I thought so, but she ate too much and threw up all over her favorite outfit."

"Oh yuk," Joe said.

I lowered my eyes. "She had a bad day. Mom and Dad grounded me for a whole week."

"You got off easy!" Joe said.

"Okay Joe, back to our current problem. We might not be able to get up the stairs, but any minute now Becky is going to work up the courage and come down the stairs. We have to get Becky to carry us back up."

Joe scratched his head. He pointed at me. "That makes sense but I have a couple of problems with that." He held up a finger. "ONE, we are TWO INCHES TALL! She may not see us and might accidentally squash us. TWO, she may squash us thinking we are weird bugs. THREE, she may know who were are and squash you just because, well, she does have problems with you."

I considered what Joe said. Those were all good points. I tapped my foot to help me think. I had it. "We'll hitch a ride up with something Becky loves."

"Honey, the hamster!" Joe said.

We turned and raced to the hamster cage. Not sure why we didn't think of this sooner. Joe and I just needed to slip into the cage. My dear sweet little sister would then carry us upstairs.

Running as fast as our little legs could carry us, Joe asked, "How will Honey feel about sharing her cage with us? How do we know she won't eat us?"

"Hamsters don't eat people!" I said.

"Even little people?"

"Yes Joe, even little people."

Reaching the cage, we tried to slip in through the bars, but even being two inches small was still not small enough to slip in or out of the cage.

"Man this is a good cage!" Joe said.

We heard Becky finally pounding down the last half of the stairs. She made such a racket she actually shook the basement as she jumped from stair to stair. All the while she sang:

"JINGLE BELLS
MY SISTER BELLA SMELLS
SHE SMELLS SO BAD
IT MAKES ME SAD
EACH AND EVERY DAY.
I HAVE TO SAY
HEY HEY HEY
JINGLE BELLS
BELLA SO SMELLS
SHE MAKES ME YELL!
JINGLE BELLS
BELLA SO SMELLS..."

The song repeated that verse a lot.

Joe listened and smiled. "She has a nice voice and the song is catchy." He paused, "But boy, she really doesn't like you!"

"She does," I insisted. "It's just the basement that really scares her." I pointed to the cage. "Come on, we have to get in here pronto!"

"Oh nice use of Spanish!" Joe said.

I looked over the lock on the door. As a normal sized human I had never really paid it much attention. I could easily flip up the latch that held the door snug, with my little finger. But now the latch happened to be just out of my reach, even if I stood on my tiptoes and jumped.

"Remember what we tried to do on the stairs?" I asked Joe.

"Yep, it was like three minutes ago and such an epic fail it would be hard to forget."

I pointed at the latch. "But we can learn from that. I can boost you up on my shoulders and you can flip the latch!"

Joe looked at the latch. "How about I boost you up? I really don't want to fall or fart on you twice in the same hour…"

I patted him on the back, "Sure."

Joe positioned himself by the cage door. He bent down. I sat on his shoulders. He stood up. I rose with him. Sure enough I was now on the same level as the latch. I reached forward and flipped the latch. The door popped open.

"We did it!" I shouted. I waved my arms in victory! I fell over banging my head against the cage.

Joe laughed. "Sorry! But it was funny."

I had to admit that it was. I leapt to my feet. I pointed towards the stairs. Becky had finally made her way down. She approached slowly though. Like she was afraid to step on glass.

"Man, you really scared this poor girl!" Joe said.

I pulled the cage door open. "In!" I ordered.

Joe pulled himself up into the cage. I followed

him, then pulled the cage door closed.

Honey walked over to us. I held my hands out. "Nice Honey! Nice Honey!"

Honey sniffed me. She sniffed me again. She stuck out her tongue. She turned and walked away.

"Wow, I think you just got dissed by a hamster!" Joe told me.

I lifted my arm and sniffed myself. "I don't smell that bad!"

We saw Becky wandering over towards us, slowly. Of course she talked with each step.

"Okay, here I come...."

"Bella, you'd better not be trying to scare me!"

"Bella, you'd better not be hurting my poor little Honey!"

"Honey is sweet; Honey is always there for me!"

Joe looked at me. "Man she likes her hamster better than you."

I nodded. "She is a sweet hamster."

"So should we shout to Becky? Get her to notice us?"

I thought about it for a second or two. "No, Becky might think this is some sort of mean trick, or be scared or something. It's best we hide and just let her take us up the stairs."

Joe looked left and right. "We're in a hamster cage! Where do we hide? On the spinning wheel thing?"

I pointed to some crumbled up papers all over the cage. "Under those...."

Joe frowned. I don't see Joe frown a lot. "Doesn't Honey poop and wee there?"

I headed towards the corner of the cage. "Not if we go really close to the corner." I pulled a reluctant Joe with me. "Come on."

"Stop! Stop! Freeze!" Joe shouted.

"What?" I asked.

Joe pointed at a giant poop right under my foot. "Ah you almost buried your foot in poop."

Phew, that would have been nasty. Hamster poop may be little and cute when you are people size, but when you are peanut size, not so much. Joe and I navigated carefully around the poop to the corner of the cage.

Looking over my shoulder I saw Becky lumbering towards us.

"There you are my dear sweet Honey!" she said.

Joe and I dived under the paper pieces.

Becky finally reached the cage. "How could that smelly belly stinky binky Bella leave you down here all alone?" Becky stomped a foot that rattled the cage. "That Bella makes me so so mad!"

"Yeah good thing we hid under the smelly paper," Joe whispered to me. "Your sister is not a fan."

"It's a phase she's going through," I whispered back.

Becky bent down and tapped the cage. The sound vibrated through Joe and I. I wondered if maybe Becky suspected we were shrunken and in the cage. No, no way she could have believed that. Nobody would believe that.

"The good news my little Honey, is that mom says I can get a bright new blue cage for you! It has the latest stuff that any hamster would love. The floor is comfier. The wheel less squeaky! The mirror is super shiny! All your hamster friends will be so jealous of you!"

"Hamster friends?" Joe whispered to me.

"What can I say? My sister is a little strange."

We felt the cage being lifted off the ground by Becky. We had made progress! We were finally getting out of the basement!

Chapter 7

Becky carried us up the stairs. I heard Mom say, "Becky could you help me outside for a moment!"

"Oh, Mom, why can't you get Bella to help you?" Becky moaned.

"Don't worry, I will have plenty for her to do as well," Mom insisted. "Remember today's the day of our yard sale."

"But Mom! I love our yard now that it doesn't stink anymore!" Becky cried. "I don't want to sell our yard."

I could hear the smile in Mom's voice. "Honey, we've been through this before. We are not selling the yard. We are using our yard to sell old items that we don't use or need anymore."

"Oh right!" Becky said, more upbeat. "Can we sell Bella's old socks? Those things really stink."

"No honey, we only sell things that people will want. I think we can all agree; NOBODY wants Bella's old socks!" Mom laughed.

"My socks don't stink!" I whispered to Joe.

"No, no, of course they don't," Joe said. From his tone I could tell he really didn't quite mean that.

"Wait, are you telling me my socks do smell?" I asked Joe.

Joe rolled his eyes. "Bella, we're two inches tall and hiding under pee filled paper in a hamster cage, we have bigger things to worry about!"

"Right," I agreed. "But my socks don't smell. At least not more than any other socks,"

"By the way, Becky have you seen Bella?" Mom asked.

Becky shook her head, shaking our cage. "Nah, I've been lucky so far." She lifted the cage. "She left poor Honey down in the basement all alone! I'm going to take her back to my room where she'll be safe!"

"Actually honey, I need you outside right now," Mom told Becky.

"You talking to me or my hamster?" Becky asked.

"I'm talking to you, but your hamster can come too. The fresh air will be good for her!" Mom said.

Joe turned his head to me. "I have a question?"

"Yes, Joe?"

"Why the heck are we still hiding? Your mom is the brilliant scientist and super inventor genius. She can see us, save us and zap us back!"

Joe had an amazing point. I had been so concerned with not freaking out Becky, and then the fact that my socks didn't smell, that I had missed the big picture.

"Let's go!" I said, starting to push myself up.

Sadly, the bottom of the cage happened to be covered with something very sticky.

"I'm stuck!" I told Joe.

Joe tried to push up. "Ah, I'm stuck too…"

We could feel the cage moving. We heard Becky whining, "Why do I have to help when Bella doesn't? I hope it's not too sunny outside. I don't have my sun block on! You sure we can't sell Bella's socks? We can sell them to people we don't like! Wait, what do you mean stuff I don't use? I use all my stuff! Are you sure Honey will be okay outside? She's an inside hamster."

Blocking the whining out of my mind, I turned to Joe. "We have to stand up!"

Joe rolled his eyes. "Well, duh!"

I shot him a look.

"Sorry," Joe said slowly, "But that was kind of obvious. Of course we need to stand…"

"Is there any part of you that's not sticky?" I asked.

I looked at Joe. He moved his head up and down. "My head." He moved his legs up and down. "My legs! I can move my legs!" He grinned at me. "What about you?"

I rolled my head. I kicked my legs. "The same!" I said. "We can work with this."

"Right!" Joe said. His eyes opened wide. "How?"

I ran the ideas through my mind. We could push really hard with our hands. But no, whatever this sticky stuff was, it seemed to be too strong for us to push away from. I tried not to think about what that sticky stuff could be. I did know it had to be icky, very icky. Okay, mind off that for now. We needed to stand without using our hands. "We have to do a butt stand!" I said.

Joe looked at me with his eyes crossed. "Huh? You lost me…"

"We have to use our butts. They're a strong muscle!" I insisted. "We need to spin over on our backs and stand up using our legs. We did this in gym class when we did yoga week."

"I admit I didn't enjoy that lesson," Joe told me.

"Still we learned how to do this…I'll spin right, you spin left!" I told Joe.

I concentrated on my shoulders. I pulled up with my right shoulder, pulling my body over to the left. At first the sticky floor fought to keep my body stuck to it, but I forced my shoulder up. I rolled to my side and let momentum carry me to my back.

"I did it!" I shouted. Now looking upwards at the cage ceiling, I turned my head to see Joe now also on his back.

"I feel like a turtle," Joe said. "And not in a good way." He took a deep breath; I guess he remembered that much from yoga class. "Now what?" he asked.

"We sit up!" I said. "Duh!" I added. To show him what I meant (even if it should have been obvious) I put my hands in front of me and did a sit up.

"Oh!" Joe said. "I can do that!" He put his hands behind his head and sat up. "Tada!" he said with a smile. "We're half way there!"

"Now we pull our legs in and stand up!" I told Joe.

I did as I told him. I bent my knees and pulled my legs into my waist. I shot my legs outwards. I stood, using my arms for balance. I turned and gave Joe a grin. "Easy peasy!"

Joe looked forward. He pulled his legs back. He tried to gain momentum to stand. He succeeded in rocking back and forth on his back. But he didn't rise to his feet. He held up a finger. "I got this!" He rocked back and forth, back and forth. He held his arms! He stood up sort of. He fell back down.

I walked over and offered my hand. "Here, let me help you."

Joe looked up at me and grinned. "Oh right, you're already standing!"

Joe took my hand. I put my other hand on his shoulder, I bent over and pulled him up.

We had done it! We had stood up! Okay, I know what you're probably thinking, *big deal, you've just managed to stand up on your feet. You're still two inches tall and in a hamster cage*. I couldn't argue with you. But when you are two inches tall, you take any victory that you can.

Not only did it feel good about standing up, but the cool air felt good in our face. Oh my goodness! We were outside now! Joe and I had been so involved with trying to stand up that we hadn't noticed we were outside. We were sitting on a table with a bunch of junk mom had been hoping to sell to our neighbors in our junk, I mean yard sale.

"We're outside!" I said to Joe.

He shook his head. "Well duh!" He dropped his head. "Sorry."

"Nah, no problem, buddy. I deserved that. I've given you enough duhs today."

The sun shining down on us seemed a bit extra warm. I didn't know if it was because we were two inches tall, or in a metal cage. I did know we had to get out of this cage and back to regular size. I saw Mom across the yard giving some directions to Becky.

"Becky, I want to organize this yard sale in a logical order," Mom said.

Becky meanwhile, was searching through a box that contained her old dolls. She picked up a doll with its hair all over the place. "Wait, I still play with this one!" Becky insisted.

Mom bent over and looked her in the eyes. When Mom looked you in the eyes, it was hard to lie to her. "Really?" Mom asked.

Becky sank back. "I might. You never know. I mean Barbette used to be my favorite doll. I talked to her a lot. She always agreed with me. She thinks I'm the best and Bella is the worst and smells bad," Becky grinned. "But all my dolls think that. I have the smartest dolls!"

Mom nodded. "Yes, yes you do. That's why I want to give some of these away to charity. This way, poor kids who don't have a lot of dolls can have a nice doll to play with."

"Fine, as long as they get a good home!" Becky said.

Joe walked over to me. He pointed to me. "Can I suggest we try to shout to your mom now? Or maybe somebody else? Then they can tell your mom and she can fix this!"

Chapter 8

Joe had a great point. A few people had already shown up for the yard sale. This seemed to be the time to get out of this cage and attract attention. I pointed to the cage door.

"Let's move!"

Joe and I popped open the cage gate. Apparently Honey had been waiting for us to do this. Becky always insisted Honey was a clever hamster that was smarter and better smelling then me. Becky was right. Honey bolted to the door knocking us over. I flew out of the cage onto a hard surface. Joe crashed face first into the floor of the cage.

"Ow, that really hurt!" Joe moaned from the floor. "Just glad I missed the poop."

"Come on Joe! Up Up Up!" I told him.

Joe pushed himself up. "Yes coach," he said.

I helped Joe out of the cage. We now stood on a table surrounded by boxes of stuff. Stuff that mom had planned to put on this table but hadn't got around to yet.

Scanning the area for Mom, I saw her on the other side of the yard near the front door. She had a couple more boxes in her hand and Becky following close behind whining away.

"Mom! Mother!! Mommy!!! You can't sell my old clothing! I know you say they don't fit any more but what if something happened and I became young again, then those clothes would fit again!" Becky offered.

I looked at Joe. "Sometimes that girl can be so

ridiculous."

Joe waved a finger at me. "In this house any thing is possible!"

"Good point," I admitted. "Now, let's get Mom's attention."

We started jumping up and down, waving and making all the noise we could.

"Mom! Mom!!! MOOOOOOOOM!" I screamed at the top of my lungs.

"One plus one equals four! One thousand is less than one million! The sun rises in the west! The Earth is flat!! The sun is cold! Dinosaurs still exist!! The moon is made of cheese! Green plus Blue makes Pink!"

I stopped my yelling and turned to Joe. "Why are you yelling that?"

Joe crossed his arms. "You know how your mom loves science and science stuff. I figure if she hears wrong science facts she'll respond to it. She can't help it. She's a born teacher."

Actually Joe had a good point. Not a great point. But still Mom did seem to always sense when somebody said something wrong about science, and she always felt the need to correct them. A couple of weeks ago, I mentioned how Pluto was a planet, and Mom gave me a looooong talk about the difference between planets and dwarf planets.

I joined in the shouting of wrong things:
"Oxygen is bad for you!!!"
"Gravity is a hoax!"
"The Sun rotates around the Earth!!"
"Thunder is nature farting!!"
"Only boys can be scientists!"
Joe looked at me, "Oh that's a good one!"

We looked over at Mom who was looking at Becky. Despite our best efforts, our tiny voices were not being heard over Becky's normal sized whines.

Suddenly Becky stopped whining to mom. She turned to our table. "Honey is loose!" she screamed.

Joe turned to me. "It's like she and that hamster share a mind."

Yeah it was kind of uncanny, the link Honey and Becky had. Becky seemed to almost always know where her hamster was, and what Honey was thinking. I swear at times they did think alike, only Honey was a bit smarter. After all, Honey liked me more.

Becky raced over towards us. "Yikes! Honey is on the edge of that table she could fall!!"

I turned to Joe. "See, that's where Honey is actually smarter than Becky. Honey is way too smart to fall off of a table like this. Becky isn't smart enough to understand that. If they do share a brain, Honey uses more of it."

"Keep yelling and waving!" Joe said.

"Good point!"

We both jumped up and down yelling.

"Mom! Mom!! Mom!!!! Mommy!!!!"

"Bella's mom!!! Bella's mom!!!!!!!"

Mom and Becky rushed towards our table. Sadly though, Mom had her attention locked on Becky. Becky had her attention locked on Honey. Becky ran, not caring what she knocked over on her way to her precious hamster.

"Becky honey, be careful!" Mom pleaded. "You're making a mess!"

"Honey needs me!" Becky insisted. "We can pick these things up later! Honey is more important. If she falls, she'll get hurt!"

I shook my head. "Silly little sister! A fall from this height wouldn't hurt Honey much at all. Not only is Honey smarter than you, she's tougher!"

"Boy, you and your sister have issues!" Joe told me. "Keep yelling and waving!"

I looked at him. "We love each other. We do. But we also drive each other crazy! Maybe it's because we're so much alike? I don't know."

Joe pointed at Becky closing in on us fast. "We can talk about your issue when we are big again. For now we have bigger problems!!"

I turned my attention back to Mom and Becky. But Becky was so locked onto Honey that she didn't notice her big sister was now her tiny sister. Becky reached over the table and lunged for Honey. The entire table shook. Joe and I held our arms out to keep our balance and not fall off the table. I breathed a sigh of relief as we managed to hold on. Becky leaned over the table.

"Come to me, Honey!"

The table tipped towards Becky. Honey slid into Becky's arms. Joe and I slid off the table.

We screamed. But nobody could hear us over Becky's sobs of joy and Mom yelling at Becky to be careful.

The cage crashed to the ground. Joe and I, being lighter than the cage drifted a little farther. We both landed in a box that was next to the table. We found ourselves laying in the box next to a bunch of old dolls.

"Well that could have been worse!" Joe told me.

I agreed. We had fallen and survived unhurt. My guess was, we were so small the breeze current slowed our fall.

An old lady stuck her head over the box. Oh gross! From this angle we could see all the hair in the lady's nose. It looked like a jungle up there, a wild hairy jungle. Oh gross! Gross!! Gross!!

The lady had gray hair, wrinkled skin and her breath smelled of onions. She leaned over the box. "My granddaughter would love these old dolls!" she said. Some of her spit shot into the box covering Joe and I.

"Oh yuck!" I said.

"Hey!! Grandma!! Look down here!! Yoohoo!!!!!" Joe yelled.

The lid of the box closed over the opening at the top. It went dark.

"This might not be good," Joe said to me.

The box lifted up off the ground.

We heard the old lady's voice, "My granddaughter will love this!"

Chapter 9

We felt ourselves moving. We stopped. We felt ourselves drop. We heard a car door opening. We felt ourselves going up again. We dropped down again. We landed with a thud that tossed us around inside the box. Then we heard the sound of a door closing.

"I think we're in a car," Joe deduced.

We heard another door open then close. We heard the sound of an engine.

"I really think we're in a car," Joe said.

We felt ourselves being pulled away. We shot to the other side of the box.

"Yeah, this is a car! Right?" Joe said, trying to get me to respond.

"Yes Joe, either we are in a car or this is the world's fastest grandma with a bad case of indigestion!"

"Pretty sure that's a motor sputtering, not a stomach rumbling!" Joe said. "Plus, I don't think any granny could move this fast!"

I nodded in agreement. This granny drove like a psycho! We'd already shot forward in the box as she sped up, but then went flying backwards when she slammed on the brakes to stop. This grandma seemed only able to drive really fast, and then stop suddenly at the last minute. I actually worried more about being in a car crash than being two inches tall. It seemed that some good had come of this new situation. For a second I had forgotten that Joe and I were tiny and in a box of dolls.

"I'm scared!" Joe said.

"I am too! This woman drives like a crazy person!"

Joe shook his head. "Not about that! But how do we know she's not taking us hundreds of miles away! What if we never see our homes again?"

"That's not going to happen, surely this lady lives close by.

Finally, after being tossed around like a rag doll in a box for what seemed like forever, we came to a stop.

"Are we stopped for good?" Joe asked. "Please let us be stopped for good!"

I didn't let myself get my hopes up that this ride had ended. Sure we had been standing still for like a minute, which was way longer than any stop we'd made. But knowing this grandma she might have been lost. Or who knows, she might have been asleep? I didn't get a good look at the granny, but from her winkles and dry skin I figured she had to be ancient, like seventy years old. I actually was impressed that she was still driving.

"I hope I'm still driving when I'm this lady's age," I said.

Joe laughed. "That's not going to happen. By the time you're that old, cars will be driving themselves!"

"Let's just hope she's really stopped for good," I replied.

The car shot forward. "Ooops, that wasn't the brake!" the old lady giggled. The car slammed to a stop. A door opened. "Oopsie, I better turn off the car!" the lady said. The car sputtered off.

We heard a door close. We heard another door open.

"I think she's coming for us now!" Joe said.

"Very good, Sherlock!" I teased.

We felt the box lift up from seat. "Yep, she's definitely got us!" Joe said. His eyes popped open. "Unless of course your mom invented some sort of levitating box. Maybe we're still in your yard close to my home and yours?"

I fought back the urge to make fun of Joe for such a crazy idea. Okay, I gotta admit, normally that wouldn't be a crazy idea when it came to my house. After all, I have a mom who invented super poop. But we clearly had seen an old lady, heard an old lady and a car. It didn't take a genius to figure out we had traveled somewhere in a car...a very poorly driven car. But I saw Joe shaking and knew I had to do something to calm his nerves.

"Joe, the crazy grandma lady did take us somewhere. We can be pretty sure of that. Now she has stopped the car and I think it's safe to say she's delivering us to her granddaughter. But the good news is we can't be that far away from our houses. We only drove for a short time. I'm also certain whoever finds us will be able to take us back to my mom, and then my mom can zap us back into normal size."

Joe breathed a little sigh of relief. "Phew."

I'm glad he believed me. Now I just had to hope I was right!

Chapter 10

We heard the little old grandma's footsteps. We could hear her panting a bit. In between her pants, we heard her say things like.

"This box is heavier than I thought!"

"My, I'm getting old."

"Oh my knees aren't what they used to be."

"Still, it will be good to see the smile this puts on my dear sweet little Meg's face."

"I'm such a good granny."

She came to a stop. We heard a knock on the door. We heard her tapping her foot impatiently. She shook us in the box. Not sure why she did that, but it tossed us around.

She rang the doorbell once, and then again and again.

"This box is getting heavier," Grandma sighed.

"Actually, the box is the same weight!" Joe pointed out. "She's just getting tired."

I stopped myself from rolling my eyes and saying something snappy like, "Nice job, Captain Science."

We heard the door open. A young girl screamed with excitement. "Granny! How great it is to see you!! Is that for me? Is it? Is it?? Is it???"

We felt Granny nod. "Sure is honey. I was slowly driving by a yard sale and stopped. Because you know me, I love a good yard sale. Like I always say, another person's junk is my treasure. But I saw this box of toy dolls and said to myself, Granny you have to get this for

Meg.

"Wow!!!!!" Meg screamed.

We felt ourselves lower. We felt Granny hand us over to Meg.

We rocked back and forth, side to side, as Meg shook the box hard. Not really sure why she felt she needed to do that.

"What's in it? What's in it?" Meg shouted jumping up and down. Joe and I hit the top of the box and then fell back down…up, down, up down.

"Can you get seasick in a box?" Joe asked turning

a bit gray.

I felt my stomach flip inside out. "Maybe not seasick, but definitely box sick." I fought back the urge to throw up. I smiled, that would have been quite the surprise for little Meg when she opened this box!

Meg continued to jump up and down like crazy. "Now I know how a tossed salad feels," Joe said.

We heard Meg cry, "Can I take this upstairs to show the boys?"

"Of course, go and show your brothers," Grandma replied.

"Yippee!!!" Meg shouted. She jumped up and down a few more times. The jumping stopped. We felt ourselves moving. We heard footsteps racing up some stairs.

"What's the plan?" Joe asked me.

"This Meg girl seems really excitable," I sighed.

"Yep, I got that too!" Joe said.

"When she opens the box, stay stiff and pretend to be a toy. We need to find somebody calm to explain our situation to. Then they can call my mom and all will be well!" I said. "Easy."

Joe squinted at me with a tilted head. "Easy? I don't think anything is easy when you are two inches tall."

"Okay, not easy, but we can do this! We're two smart kids!"

Joe scratched his head. "I don't think two smart kids would have gotten themselves shrunk, and then trapped in a box and delivered across town to a really excitable girl."

"I didn't say we were REALLY smart. We're just kind of smart, and daring. So we make little mistakes now and then, all in the name of science," I said in my most serious voice.

Joe looked at me in silence.

"Come on Joe!" I coaxed. "Now is not the time to stop believing in me!" I smiled. "Any kids clever enough to get themselves shrunk can figure out a way to get unshrunk."

Joe walked forward and patted me on the shoulder. "Sorry for doubting you Bella!"

We felt the box stop moving. We heard a door open. Meg said, "Zac! Zac! Look at these cool toys Grandma brought me!"

"How does she know we're cool toys?" Joe asked. "She hasn't even looked yet."

"She's assuming!" I said.

Hearing the name Zac was weird. Because, well…Zac is the name of the best looking boy in my class, the one I have a huge crush on. Heck he's probably the best looking boy in the school, if not the town, if not the world! He has dark messy hair, dreamy eyes and a smile as bright as the sun. No. No way this could be Zac's house. The world isn't that cruel to me, where it would shrink me and deliver a two-inch me to Zac's house.

The cover popped off the box. Joe and I had to squint because of the bright light. Looking down on us, I saw a pair of familiar dreamy eyes and a familiar amazing smile. Oh man, this was bad.

Chapter 11

No! No! A thousand million times, NO! I could not have Zac see me like this. Forget that I was two inches tall, I was wearing old clothing and so dirty from being close to the ground and stuck in a hamster's cage. Nope. I'd rather stay small forever than have Zac see me like this. How can this have possibly happened? In normal circumstances, I'd love to be visiting Zac at his house. It would be a dream come true. But not like this. Not when I've been reduced to the size of a cockroach and am clinging furiously onto the dress of one of his sister's dolls.

This couldn't get any worse. Could it? Of course it could. Joe started waving his arms and yelling, "Hey, look down here!"

I elbowed Joe in the gut. He bent over and more importantly went quiet.

"Why the heck did you do that?" he groaned. "Zac can save us! He has a cell phone. He can call your home, talk to your mom and we can get back to normal!"

"Quiet!" I ordered. "I don't want to be saved like this. We'll be the laughing stock of the entire school, if not the world! We're a viral video just waiting to happen!"

"I'd rather be a laughing stock than squashed!" Joe told me.

But Joe knew about my crush. He stopped and thought about this. "Get real, Bella! Being saved is much more important than your crush on some boy from school. Yeah sure, he's probably the coolest and most popular kid in the grade and all, but seriously, Bella, we need to put things into perspective. If not, we might be crushed!" he scolded me.

Joe started jumping up and down and waving again. I tackled him. Yeah, not the most mature or smart thing to do. But like I said, no way did I want Zac to see me like this. My hair had to be a total mess, and besides, I was two inches tall! I put my hand over Joe's mouth. "Joe we will figure out another way! I promise!"

Joe pulled my hand off of his mouth. "Look Bella, you're my best friend and normally I wouldn't do this. But face it, we're not good at figuring things out. If we were, we wouldn't be TWO INCHES TALL!"

Joe shouted. "Hey, Zac! Down here! Woo hoo! Down here!"

The good news was, we were so tiny and Meg was so loud that Joe's cries could not be heard. Plus, looking up at Zac, I could see that he really was paying far more attention to his phone than to what was inside the box. He acted polite towards his sister, but any kid over the age of five would be able to tell that he didn't care about her toys. Zac was so cool.

"Kids, come down stairs, Grandma is leaving!" A voice called out to Zac and Meg. I assumed it was their mom. How lucky was that lady to be able to see Zac every day!

We felt the box drop. We hit the ground hard. We flew around a bit, but we didn't get hurt. I guess that was an advantage of being so small and cushioned by a heap of dolls.

I listened to the footsteps of Joe and his sister leaving the room. I heard a door close behind them.

"Phew! That was close!" I said.

Joe just shook his head. "Yep, it would certainly have been a shame if somebody saved us," he replied, an annoyed expression on his face.

I stood there, my arms crossed. I glared at Joe. Joe dropped back a step. "Look Bella, I get it, you like this guy. He's cool and he's a good guy, but here's the thing, you have no chance at getting him at all."

"What? Why are you saying that? Joe I thought you were my friend!" I shouted.

He held up a finger. "Wait, let me finish. You have no chance of making him like you, if you are two inches tall. I mean come on, that's just not going to work."

I nodded. "True, but I'm not planning on staying two inches tall. I just figure there's got to be another way to get back to our normal height, that doesn't involve letting Zac know that I shrunk myself."

"And me," Joe added.

I nodded, again. "Right, that too. We can get out of this ourselves. We can walk home and contact Mom."

Joe rolled his eyes. "One, we don't know how far away from home we are..."

I cut him off before he could say anything more. "We're at 33 Sun Drive, just four blocks away from my home. It's a nice fifteen-minute walk."

Joe sighed. "Really," he said slowly. "I was unaware that you knew that," he paused. "That's a little creepy, Bella."

I shook my head. "I like to go for a jog sometimes. It's good for my lungs. I may try out for the track team next year!" I said defensively.

Joe held up his hand to stop me from going on. "Also, fifteen minutes' normal size, means way more than fifteen minutes when we are two inches tall!"

I thought about it. That did make some sense. "Yeah, but we can do it. We're young and strong."

"We're also very easy to step on. Plus, we are a potential meal for any hungry bird that flies over."

"Birds don't eat people, Joe!"

"That's because most people are way bigger than birds!" Joe said.

"Your point?" I asked.

Joe shook his head, rolled his eyes and sighed. "If we get eaten and or squashed...there goes any chance you have of ever being noticed by Zac!"

I took in Joe's words. I had to admit they made sense. I had to suck it up, we needed to get to my mom and have her unshrink us. Hopefully she could unshrink us. That was all that mattered at the moment. Even if this meant embarrassing myself in front of Zac. I couldn't risk getting stepped on. After all, this wasn't just about me. Joe was also in danger here. Friends don't let friends stay small and get squashed.

"Okay, Joe, let's get out of this box and out of here!" I said with a fist pump.

Joe lifted his hand for a high five. I gave him a slap!

Joe looked up and around. "So how do we get out of this box?"

Man, when I woke up this morning, I never thought my trick for the day would be figuring out a way to get out of a box. Life sure is funny. Especially when your mom is a whacky scientist.

I looked around. "We'll use our teamwork again!" I told Joe. "We'll push a few dolls against the side of the box, stack them up and climb out."

Joe and I searched for the dolls that looked to be the easiest to move. We noticed an old Barbie doll near the side wall. I moved to it and gave it a push. It budged but not a lot. Joe came over and helped. Bending our knees and putting our backs into it, we slid the Barbie up tight against the side. Joe pointed to an old troll doll with long white hair. We grabbed the troll doll and with some effort, hoisted it up on top of the Barbie.

Joe had the idea of maybe cutting off the dolls hair and using it as a rope, which may have worked, except of course we had nothing to cut it with. So we went with the stack and climb.

Much to my surprise, we were pretty easily able to climb up on the Barbie, onto the troll and then grab the top of the box.

"Lucky that our gym teacher, Mr. Johnson, makes us do pull ups in class!" Joe said, pulling himself up onto the edge of the box.

He put one leg on the other side of the box and reached down for me. I took Joe's hand, he pulled me up. We both fell over the side and hit the ground with a splat. Good thing the room had nice thick carpet.

From the ground, Joe laughed. "That actually worked out better than I thought it would!"

Chapter 12

Looking around the room, it seemed to be a fairly average little girl's bedroom. In other words, everything was fluffy and pink. Even the carpet was thick and pink! This room was grand...suitable for a princess. Yep, when I was five or six, this would have been my dream bedroom.

Joe spent less time checking out the decor of the room. He immediately started looking for the door. It wasn't hard to find. After all, it was a door and had to be in the middle of one of the four walls. I was actually more interested in finding out more about Meg, and exploring this magnificent bedroom.

From what I gathered, Meg appeared to be a very average five or six-year-old. She was much like my sister Becky, except Meg really liked her big brother. Well I mean, who could blame her? After all, her brother was Zac! The most handsome kid in the school, if not the world.

Joe looked at me. He shook his head. "You're thinking about Zac again! Aren't you?"

"Nope, not at all," I told him. "I'm thinking how this girl loves fancy pink stuff."

Joe looked around. "Reminds me of your room a while back. Only this room is really over the top!"

I nodded. "Yeah, I did go through a pink stage. But my room never looked like this!"

Joe took my hand and gave me a pull. He pointed towards the door, which was left open just a crack. "Now's our chance to get out of here and find somebody to help us!"

"You're right!" I said, focusing on the matter at hand. That was when I started pulling Joe. "Come on Joe, let's get out of here!"

We headed quickly towards the door, moving as fast as our little legs could take us. We'd finally caught a break! Meg had left the door open a crack. It wasn't a big crack, but this was one of the few advantages of being tiny. We could easily get through the crack.

Just as we arrived at the door, we heard little feet scrambling at us. Let me correct that, little paws racing towards us.

We heard a "grrr ruff ruff!" coming loudly in our direction.

Peeking through the crack of the door, I saw a pug dog running at us. His tongue was hanging out and he looked hungry. I knew this type of dog, a little dog with a big attitude. The type of dog that would love to throw his weight around, except that he really didn't have much weight. He'd yap his head off at big dogs, challenging them. Of course big dogs would ignore him, knowing they could swat him away like a bug. Big dogs were cool like that.

But this dog had mischief in his eyes. Finally, he had somebody or something he could intimidate and tower over. I could tell this was the moment that this particular dog had been waiting his entire life for.

Joe and I threw ourselves back into the room.

The dog poked his snout through the small crack in

the doorway. He growled and drooled.

Joe and I put our weight on the door. We had to make sure this dog didn't get in. I had no interest in being pug chow! He tried to push his flat nose through the crack. He growled, tossing dog spit all over the room. Yet he couldn't break through the crack in the door. I don't think it was because of Joe and I, it's just that he was a tiny dog and the door did not appear to swing open easily. It seemed fixed in place and would need a good push to open it. Although, the dog towered over us, he didn't seem strong enough to push the door open.

The dog yapped and yapped at the door. He then concentrated on the small gap between the bottom of the door and the floor. He stuck his slimy pink tongue through, probing around and soaking the carpet. The dog kept pushing and pushing. He stuck a paw in at the side and waved it around. His paw loomed over me. I ducked or it might have taken my head off.

"Man, this dog is stubborn," Joe said. "Or hungry," he added.

Well whichever reason was causing the dog to persist, neither was very good for us. I thought about our situation. I figured this pug wasn't an extra vicious dog, he just saw something that was out of the ordinary and wanted to investigate so he could scare it off.

I started towards the crack in the doorway. Joe grabbed my arm. He pulled me back. "What are you doing?" Joe asked.

"I'm going to go and reason with the dog. Dogs are smart. He'll be able to tell I'm a human, and most dogs like humans. Dogs do not eat humans."

"That may be because no other humans are two inches tall! Have you forgotten!"

I pulled away. Yeah, Joe might have a point. But I knew that even at two inches tall, I could still convince the dog I was a human and that dogs obeyed humans.

I stood in front of the dog. His head poked through the opening. I could see his nostrils. He yapped and yapped.

I raised my hand. "Stop, dog!" I ordered.

Much to my surprise, the dog stopped yapping. He looked down at me with a tilted head; his little doggy brain trying to make logic out of what he saw. I figured I'd help show him who was in control.

"Listen dog, we're people. You're a dog! Therefore, you will obey us! Sit!" I ordered.

The dog went quiet for a second. He tilted his head the other way. He whined a little. He shivered. I could tell he'd been thinking about what I had said. I had gotten to him. This was going to work.

I waved at the dog. "Go away!" I shouted.

He stood there. Head looking down at me, tongue wagging.

"Go!" I shouted! I reinforced my words with a stomp of my foot.

The dog started barking and yelping while trying to force his way back into the room. I jumped to the side. I stumbled and fell on the floor. Joe came over and helped me up. "I think you scared him!"

I sighed. "Yeah, I got that."

"So do you have a backup plan?" Joe asked.

"No, of course I don't!" I said turning red. I pointed to my face. "Does this look like the face of a person who has a backup plan? A person with a backup plan wouldn't let themselves be shrunken to two inches!" I shouted.

Joe looked me in the eyes. He put his hands on my shoulders. "Look Bella, we messed up. We messed up BIG time!" He laughed. "Ha, kind of funny that messing up big time made us SMALL."

"Get to the point, Joe!"

"Right. Even though we messed up. We're still two really smart kids! Yeah, sometimes we may do ridiculous things without thinking about consequences. But we can always find a way to fix whatever we did wrong. That's what we have to do now. We have to concentrate on a solution. I know we can do this. After all, we're Bella and Joe - the great science adventurers. This is just another adventure."

While Joe talked, the pug barked his foolish head off.

"Yap yap yap" over and over.

I turned and looked at the dog. "Oh be quiet!" I yelled in my most commanding voice.

The dog made a little whimper and quickly disappeared from the doorway. Had I done it? Had I finally shown that silly pooch that I'm the boss? I waited a second or two to see if he poked his head back in. Nope. I had done it! I rock!

We heard Meg's voice, "Silly Mr. Puggy why were you making so much noise?"

We heard Mr. Puggy whimper a bit.

"We almost got eaten by something called Mr. Puggy," I groaned.

"Look Bella, big picture here. We have Meg right outside the door. Do you think we should try to communicate with her?"

I thought about it. We needed to make contact with somebody. Somebody who could call my house and my mom. But something told me hyper excitable Meg wouldn't be our best choice. I couldn't be sure how she would react to two little people in her room.

Okay, think Bella, I told myself. You're a smart girl. You can figure out the best way to get out of this. After all, we just need to work out who will be the best person in this house to communicate with. I had it! It came surprisingly easy.

I nudged Joe. "We have to get to Zac."

"Say what? Come again?" Joe replied.

"I know Zac loves to read science fiction. He'll understand what happened to us. He'll contact my mom for us and then we'll be saved."

Joe looked at me. "Agreed. I have to admit Bella, I'm kind of surprised you've changed your mind about Zac seeing you like this."

"Joe, even when I'm little, I'm a big person!" I told him.

The truth was, I was kind of betting that if my crush saved us, we would then always have a common bond. I could remind him he was the one who could see us when no one else could. He would become my hero. Yeah, I might look (and smell) terrible today. But he would forget about that as he'd be more concerned with the bigger picture. We would become friends through this adventure we'd shared. Our friendship could then bloom into something more. Would it happen immediately? No. But I had time. This was a long-term plan. A plan that I knew could work.

"You're thinking that somehow this will make you closer to Zac," Joe stated with a nod of his head.

Joe knew me so well. "No no, of course not," I replied.

Joe just looked at me, tapping his foot.

"Maybe," I admitted. "But it still makes sense. Zac knows us. He knows my mom is a whacky scientist. He loves science. We can make this happen. We only need to find Zac's room. Then we talk to him, nice and calm like. It's the perfect plan."

Joe nodded. "It's not a perfect plan, but it is a plan that's better than most of our plans."

The door swung open. Meg walked in with Mr. Puggy in her arms. "Good Mr. Puggy. Glad to see you've finally quietened down."

Joe pointed to her, though he really didn't need to. "Now we just need to avoid being squashed by a giant six-year-old!"

"That's easy!" I said. "Follow me!"

I moved carefully towards Meg, timing her steps. With Mr. Puggy in her arms she was moving slowly, left foot then right foot. All we needed to do was shoot between her legs. The way she was holding Mr. Puggy in front of her meant she wouldn't be able to see us if we passed directly under her.

"Now!" I told Joe, grabbing his hand and pulling him.

We ran under her raised left foot.

Mr. Puggy must have noticed us, as he started to grumble and growl.

"Mr. Puggy calm down!" Meg told him. "I don't know why you're so excited today!"

We made it past the left foot just as it touched the ground. The right foot lifted off the ground. We raced under the right foot. We had clear sailing to the door!

We made it to the hallway! We had done it.

Chapter 13

The thick gray hallway carpet felt nice under our feet, but it did make it harder for us to move fast. We counted five doors. We figured one bathroom and four bedrooms. That meant one for Zac, one for his parents and one for Meg. Was the fourth bedroom a spare or for another sibling?

We made our way along the hallway.

"Does Zac have any other brothers or sisters?" Joe asked me.

"How should I know?" I answered far more defensively than I intended.

"You seem to know A LOT about him," Joe answered calmly.

I inhaled. "Sorry, in all my hikes around here I never noticed any siblings, including Meg."

"Fair enough," Joe said.

We heard the clatter of feet running up the stairs. Turning, we saw two little kids racing around. One of the kids had dark curly hair and was chasing another little kid who looked like a very young version of Zac.

The chasing kid reached for the little Zac look-alike. "Tag! Got you, Bobby! You're it!!" he shouted.

Bobby stopped and stomped a foot playfully. "I'm going to get you, Trent!"

Bobby raced at Trent who had a good lead on him. Bobby didn't seem to care. In fact, from the look of joy on his face, it didn't look like Bobby cared much about anything, except for playing and having a good time. Oh to be a young child again, with no worries and problems!

Joe and I pinned ourselves up against the hall wall, as the two little kids took turns chasing each other. Their faces were covered with sweat but they didn't seem to mind. One would run until he hit the door at the end of the hall, the other would tag him. Then they would reverse. They did this about ten times, each time becoming rougher and making more noise.

A voice called from downstairs, "Bobby what are you and Trent doing up there?"

"Nothing, Mom!" Bobby shouted back innocently.

"Yeah nothing!" Trent shouted back in agreement.

"I have some more cookies and milk for you boys!" the voice from downstairs called.

Their faces lit up. "Coming Mom!" Bobby cried.

The two tore down the stairs.

"I don't know if those two kids need any more sugar," Joe said.

"Agreed, but for now they are out of our way. Now to find Zac!"

We moved steadily towards the stairs. The good news was, unlike the stairs in my basement, these had carpet on them. If we slipped we wouldn't get hurt, at least not too much. Still, there were a lot of them to get down.

"Should we try the stairs?" I asked.

Joe looked down the steep incline. "It won't be easy."

We heard the little kids' voices, "Thanks for the cookies!"

Seconds later, Bobby and his friend started racing back towards the stairs.

"I knew these kids didn't need any more sugar!" Joe insisted.

I looked down the stairs at the two hyperactive kids in view.

"I guess the best plan is to wait for Zac in his room," I said.

Joe nodded in agreement. "Yeah, we know he needs to sleep, so we'll just have to wait. Way less chance of being eaten or stomped on."

The two little boys hit the stairs. They started racing up. Joe pulled me away. "Come on let's boogie!" he said.

"Boogie?" I asked.

He took my hand and pulled me. "Something my dad says, it means to 'move it' in old people's talk. Parents can be so weird!" Joe concluded.

We heard the kids clamoring up the stairs. Boy they were fast. No time to look for Zac's room. We headed into the first open door. The room kind of smelled of socks. I looked at the racecar shaped bed. "This must be Bobby's room!"

Joe pointed to the bed. "Under that bed is probably the safest place!"

Excellent idea. We darted under the bed. I saw the floor coated with crumbs. They actually smelled good. Until that moment I had no idea how hungry I was. "Gee, those crumbs smell good!" I said.

Joe rubbed his stomach. "Wow, I'm hungry."

We headed towards the crumbs. They smelled like old cookies. Joe grabbed a couple and shoved them into his mouth. I followed his lead. I grabbed a big crumb and started nibbling. It might just have been the tastiest thing I had ever eaten.

"You know we're eating crumbs, right?" Joe said.

"Sssh Joe, don't ruin the moment," I scolded.

We sat down and enjoyed ourselves for the first time since we'd been shrunk. Yes, we had sunk so low that eating crumbs had become the best part of our day. They were tasty! I could not complain.

I heard something. Kind of a rustling or a shuffling. Looking over my shoulder I saw a bunch of ants coming towards us. "Uh oh," I said, pointing out the ants to Joe. "Looks like we aren't the only ones who like cookie crumbs."

Chapter 14

Joe saw the ants. There had to be dozens of them. They were the small black annoying ones. As normal size people these would have been nothing to worry about. We wouldn't have even noticed them. Of course we wouldn't have been eating crumbs either. But Joe and I weren't in the mood to share, especially with a bunch of annoying ants.

"At least we're still bigger than them," I said.

"Ants are super strong!" Joe noted. "We may be bigger, but I'm betting they're stronger."

"But we're smarter!" I said. "Let's look for something we can fight them off with."

We searched around under the bed. Any kid that would litter his floor with cookies had to have lost other stuff under his bed. We'd seen Bobby in action. He didn't look like the 'everything in its place' kind of kid. Sure enough, under the bed there were some coins, lots of dust, a couple of toy soldiers and a few balls. I pointed at the balls. "Those! We can roll them at the ants!"

"My gosh, Bella! You're brilliant!"

I grinned. "It's about time you figured that out my friend."

I thought about the best way to execute our plan. One option would be for us both to roll balls at the ants and try to drive them off, or squash as many as we could. The other option would be to split the tasks, one of us rolls balls at the ants while the other collects bits of food. There appeared to be enough crumbs under this bed for both us and the ants. I guessed there was no need to get greedy. After all, we'd rather have the ants taking crumbs back to their nest, rather than taking us.

I pointed at the balls. "Joe, you're the better bowler!" I told him, even though that wasn't necessarily true. I pointed to some crumbs lining the floor near us. "I'll collect enough crumbs for us to eat, and I'll leave some for any ants that make it past the balls."

"You want to share with ants?" Joe asked.

"Yes, I do. It only seems fair. After all, they have to be small and tiny forever. We're only like this until Mom unshrinks us."

Joe stood there scratching his head, like he always did when he had to think something through.

"So, we're sharing with ants..."

"Yes, Joe, this is pretty much their picnic and we're ruining it."

Joe's eyes lit up. "Man, I never thought of it that way!" His smile faded. "In that case, maybe we should leave all the food to them? Or maybe we should just ignore them?"

I waved towards the balls. Joe had this tendency to either under think or over think things. Now he was stuck in over think mode. When he got like that, I had to be forceful.

"Joe, it's us or them," I was serious.

Joe dropped his head and headed towards the nearest ball. Just in time, as I could somehow smell the ants closing in on us. They had an odor that I had never noticed when I was big. It didn't smell bad. It just smelled different, it smelled like anxiety or something. That made me anxious.

I bent down and collected as many small crumbs

as I could, storing them in my pockets. Looking up, I saw the ants were much closer and they all seemed to be focused on us. We were their next meal!

"Roll the ball Joe!" I hollered.

I watched a ball go rolling by. The ball hit a couple of the ants. "Nice shot, Joe!" I yelled.

"Thanks!" he called back.

A couple of the ants stuck to the ball and were carried away on it. I continued with my gathering. Another ball rolled by me quickly. It missed the ants but certainly got their attention. They stopped their march towards us. They seemed to look at each other as if to say, *what the heck is going on here*? I got hit in the back with a ball. It knocked me forward to the ground and then bounced backwards.

"Oops sorry!" I heard Joe say.

I found myself surrounded by three big ants. Their antennae moved rapidly. I rolled to my feet. The ants came marching at me. My first thought was to hit them. They looked really creepy and mean. I needed a plan that didn't involve hand-to-hand combat with ants. I noticed the ball that had hit me. I shot towards it. I moved behind it and pushed the ball at the charging ants. It rolled over them. It didn't squash them, but it knocked them back. I jumped up and down waving my arms. "Shoo!!" I shouted.

"They aren't dogs!" Joe shouted.

"Animals are animals!" I said back to him.

"They aren't animals, they're insects," Joe said. "You really should pay more attention in science class."

"I'm not a bug person! But you're starting to bug me!" I told him.

I continued jumping up and down and waving my hands. "GO! GO! GO!" I screamed at the ants.

"I don't think ants can hear things," Joe said.

I knew he was probably right. But I was guessing they could sense when they weren't wanted. Not sure why I thought that, especially after all the picnics I'd been on that ants had invaded. Still I figured that ants could tell when they faced something they didn't want to mess with.

The ants actually stood there taking in the situation. Another ball rolled passed me and through the ants. The ants turned and moved back. I gathered more crumbs and headed back towards Joe.

Joe and I gave each other high fives. It's always nice when a plan works out, even if that may have been one of the few times one of our plans was successful. Thinking a bit more...it may have been the only time one of our plans had worked out. I decided best not to think too much about it and to enjoy the moment.

Joe and I sat down and munched on a few more crumbs. The ants kept their distance. A few of them collected the crumbs on the far edge from us. They were the brave ones, most of the ants just took off.

"Ha! We showed those ants who's the boss!" I told Joe.

He smiled and took a bite. "Agreed. We're pretty tough."

"Yes we are!" I said, holding up a crumb in victory.

Joe's face turned white.

"Wait, Joe what's going on?" I asked.

Joe pointed past me. "Uh oh. The ants are back with friends. Many many friends..."

Looking over my shoulder I saw an army of ants coming towards the bed. These ants looked different; much bigger, stronger and meaner!

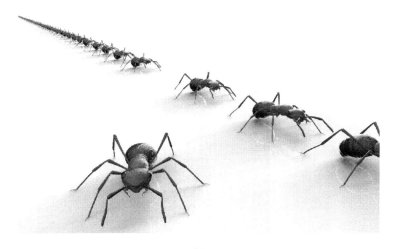

"I suggest we run!" I said.

Joe nodded. "Agreed!"

We raced out from under the bed. We caught a break, the bedspread overlapped the bed onto the floor. We climbed up the bed spread to the top of the bed. The top of the bed felt soft and comfy. Joe laid down on it.

"Wow! That was close!" he said.

"It sure was!" I replied, with a yawn.

"I'm so tired," Joe murmured.

I really hadn't noticed it until now. But yeah, I was tired too, in fact I was exhausted. And I could see that Joe felt the same way.

Chapter 15

I heard a door slam. I forced my head up from the bed and turned towards the noise. Ah, the bed felt so warm and comfy, like it was calling to me…"Come Bella, sleep!"

But when you're two inches tall, you can't sleep. Especially on the top of the bed of a young kid. A young kid who had just come bounding into his room.

I heard Bobby speak but I wasn't quite sure who he was speaking to.

I nudged Joe. "Joe get up!"

"Five more minutes please, Mom!" he said, rolling away from me.

"I'm not your mom!" I told him. I proved it to him

by pinching him on the ear.

Joe leapt up, rubbing his ear. "Why'd you do that?" he demanded.

I pointed at Bobby. Joe turned to follow my finger. His mouth dropped open. "Oh no, this is bad!"

Bobby started running towards his bed.

"I think it's about to get worse!" I shouted.

Bobby jumped into the air.

"RUN!" I yelled.

Joe and I took off in opposite directions. Bobby jumped onto the bed feet first. Okay, the kid was pretty coordinated. The bed started to shake from the force. Sadly, that was just the beginning. Bobby started to jump up and down on the bed. The bed mattress trembled and shook. Every time Bobby landed, Joe and I shot up into the air and then we would plop back down. Only to be launched again with each jump. Bobby laughed and giggled almost as much as he jumped up and down.

"Bobby! What are you doing up there?" a voice yelled from downstairs.

"Nothing!" Bobby said, as he continued leaping up and down. I saw Joe starting to turn green.

"Stop doing nothing!" the voice from downstairs shouted back.

Bobby plopped down to a sitting position. Launching Joe and I higher up than ever. Joe turned greener than ever. He lay on his stomach. I hobbled over to him.

"You don't look so good!" I said.

He groaned. "I don't feel so good either. All that sugar from the crumbs and then we just had the trampoline ride of a lifetime. He opened his mouth. He threw up. The good news was that since he was only two inches tall, his vomit hardly left a mark on the bedspread. In fact, I didn't think a normal size person would even notice it. Of course not being normal size, I certainly did notice.

I rolled Joe over, away from his vomit. "Gross!" I told him.

He burped in my face. I gagged on his breath that smelled of overly sweet sugar mixed with stomach goo. It made me want to throw up as well. I tried to fight it. I really did. I failed. I dropped to my hands and knees and everything I had eaten (yes, all those crumbs) came up.

Joe patted me on the back softly. "Feel better now?"

I looked at him. "Actually, I do."

"Me too!" Joe smiled. "Sometimes you need a good barf to clean out the system."

I groaned. I fought back the temptation to breathe my vomit breath on Joe. I didn't want to start a cycle of throwing up all over again.

A giant face appeared in front of us. "Hey, I like barfing too!" Bobby told us.

Yep, now this was different.

Chapter 16

Bobby looked at us with his mouth wide open. His breath reeked of old milk. Not pleasant at all.

"Oh hi," Joe said, giving him a little wave.

"You look funny!" Bobby told us. "What are you?"

"We're people just like you!" I told him.

Bobby shook his head. The movement rattled the bed. "No, no you're way too tiny."

"We accidently hit ourselves with a shrink ray and became small!" I said.

Bobby giggled. "You talk all funny!" he snickered, and some snot shot out of his nose. "Shrink ray! Ha! That's funny. It's like you're in a cartoon."

"Exactly!" I said.

Bobby shook his head. "Nope, not a cartoon. You don't look like a cartoon at all. You look like a very tiny person."

"We're in your brother's class," I told Bobby.

Bobby laughed and laughed. He pounded on the bed sending us flying up into the air again. He calmed down. "No, my brother is big!"

I sighed. "We should be big too! We were big until the shrink ray made us little!" I insisted.

Bobby shook his head quickly. "Nope, that makes no sense."

Joe looked at me. "He actually has us on that one."

I looked Bobby in the eyes (well more up the nose). "Look Bobby, just go and get your big brother,

Zac!"

Bobby pulled back from the bed. "How do you know my name?"

"We heard your mom call you Bobby," I said slowly.

"How do you know Zac's name?" Bobby asked.

I rolled my eyes. "I told you, we're in his class at school."

Joe leaned into me, "Be patient. Don't make him mad, he can squash us."

Bobby slapped his hand down in between us. "Ha! I can!" he shouted.

I held up both my hands. "No no no, you don't want to squash us!" I said.

Bobby looked at me. "I kind of do."

I put my hands on my hips and leaned in to him. In my sternest voice I ordered, "Bobby, I demand you go get your big brother, Zac!" Yep this is what my life had come to...I needed the coolest boy in school to save me from a slightly crazy four-year-old.

Bobby laughed and raised his arm. "Silly little bugs! I don't have to listen to you! You're tiny! You're not the boss of me! I'm the boss of me!"

Joe looked at me. "Once again he has us on that point."

I walked up closer to Bobby. "Look, Bobby, I'm not a bug!"

"You're about the size of a bug," Bobby said.

"Have you ever heard a bug talk before?" I asked.

Bobby crossed his arms and raised his chin. "Yes, yes I have!"

"Where?" I asked.

"On TV!" Bobby said. "Bugs talk all the time on

90

TV."

"Bobby, you're not making sense. Think about it. Are the bugs on TV real?"

Joe leaned into me again. "I don't think a four-year-old would know the difference between real and make believe!"

Bobby held up five fingers. "I'm five!" he spat, covering us with spit. "I just turned five yesterday! We had a party and cake and people sang to me."

"I bet they sang happy birthday!" I said.

Bobby nodded. "They did..."

"I bet you had chocolate ice cream with your cake!" I said quickly.

"I did, it made me fart!" Bobby said proudly.

"I bet people brought you presents!" I said, feeling on a roll.

Bobby nodded. "Yep. How do you know this?"

I stood up on my tiptoes. "It's a secret!" I said. I turned to Joe. "Should we tell him the secret?"

Joe looked at me with eyes and mouth wide open. He leaned into me, "I'm not sure where you're going with this," he whispered.

I turned to Bobby. "I'm a fairy princess! That's how I know all these things! Fairy princesses know everything!"

Bobby squinted at me. "Really?" He pointed at Joe. "Is he a prince?"

I shook my head. "No, he's my servant."

Joe groaned and mumbled. "Of course I'm the servant. Just once I wish I could be the prince or something."

I shot Joe a look. He stopped his complaining.

I waved my hands over my head. "Being a fairy

princess, I can do magic!" I said. "And if you help us, I can grant you one wish!"

Now Bobby crossed his arms. "How do I know you can do magic?" he asked.

"Watch!" I told him. I pointed at Joe and said. "You now think you are a dog!"

Playing along, Joe dropped to all fours and starting barking.

Bobby's eyes popped open. "Nice!" he thought for a second, which is probably about as long as Bobby had ever thought about anything. "How do I know he's not faking?"

"Watch!" I said. I popped my foot out of my shoe. I picked up my shoe and smelled it. "Yuck!" I said sticking out my tongue. I didn't need to act, the shoe smelled like three-day-old cheese.

I held my shoe out. "Dog, you will now smell my shoe!" I ordered.

Joe stood there on all fours. I looked at Bobby watching Joe. "You know, nobody would smell my shoe unless they were under a spell!" I said.

Joe slowly inched forward. He sniffed my shoe. He gagged a little. He rolled over. "Oh come on...they aren't THAT bad!" I said.

Bobby laughed and laughed. He jumped up and down. "You are magic! You are magic! Everybody knows fairies have stinky feet!"

"If that's true, then you're the fairy queen," Joe told me.

Bobby leaned into me. "I want my wish!"

I shook a finger in his face. "Not so fast. First you have to do something for me. If I'm going to grant you a wish, you have to prove that you are worthy!"

Bobby looked at me with a tilted head and slanted eyes. "Say what?"

"You do something for me and I will grant your wish!" I told him.

"Huh?" Bobby said, "You fairies talk funny."

"Bring your brother Zac to meet me and I will give you one wish!" I said slowly.

"Why Zac? Why would any fairy want to see Zac? Will you take him away and make him your prince?" Bobby asked.

"She wishes," Joe muttered under his breath.

"No," I said. "I just want to see him."

Bobby crinkled his nose. "Not sure why...will you turn him into a dog and make him sniff your shoe?" Bobby asked.

I shook my head. "Nope."

"Oh too bad," Bobby sighed. "I'd like to see that."

"Bobby, you can make that your wish!" Joe told him.

Bobby's eyes lit up. "I like that! I always wanted a pet dog!"

"Well you don't get anything unless you bring Zac to me!" I said.

Bobby bobbed his head back and forth rapidly. "Yes, yes, yep!" he said.

He reached down and picked us up.

"What are you doing? Are you going to take us to Zac?" I asked.

Bobby laughed. "No, he might try to steal the wish for himself." He carried us across the room to his desk. I saw a large aquarium filled with dirt on top of the desk. "I'm just going to keep you in my ant farm so you don't get away!" he said. "I so want my wish!"

Bobby plopped us into the dirty bowl. "Now that my ants have left it's nice to have fairies I can keep in here!" he beamed. He waved a finger over the bowl. "Now promise not to escape like my ants did. Mom will be so mad if she finds out. If I get into trouble again, I'll never get a snake like Zac!"

"We promise we'll stay right here!" I said.

Bobby looked at us through the glass. "You sure?"

"Look Bobby, a fairy promise is a golden promise!" I insisted.

Bobby smiled. "Okay, I'll go find Zac and bring him here!" Bobby turned and ran out the door yelling, "Zac!"

Joe looked at me. "So that's your plan? Have the strange five-year-old boy bring your crush, his brother to us?"

I nodded. "I think it will work."

Joe nodded. "I do too." He pointed behind me. "I just hope that big giant beetle over there doesn't mind sharing his new home with us!"

Chapter 17

The beetle we now shared a home with, crept slowly towards us. The big blue bug may have been just as tall as Joe and I. To make things even trickier it appeared to be very curious about us.

"Think it wants to be friends?" I asked Joe.

"Most beetles eat plants, but some like to eat small bugs," Joe told me.

"And our neighbor here? What does he or she prefer?" I asked.

Joe shrugged. "No idea. This is the type of thing I would normally Google. Can't really do that right now."

I pointed at the big beetle, now just inches from us.

I jumped up and down and waved my arms. "Go away! Go! Go! Go!!" I shouted at the beetle.

The beetle stopped.

"I think he's trying to figure out if you're crazy or not," Joe said. "I have an idea!"

"I'm listening…"

"Well, I do know some beetles like to eat poop."

"Oh gross, Joe!"

"And well, I haven't well, pooped in a bit and well, I kind of could you know…"

"Joe, are you telling me you need to poop?"

He rubbed his stomach. "I do. And this could kill two birds with one stone. I'd feel better, and it might draw the beetle away."

I could not believe Joe and I were standing here talking about him pooping, to lure away a giant beetle. Yep, my life had become officially extremely weird. The extra bizarre thing was this might not be a terrible idea. Of course, it could possibly be one of the worst ideas in history. But I smiled when I thought of little Bobby finding some poop in the corner of his bug house. Then again, from what I knew about Bobby, he might find that cool.

I pointed to the corner of the tank across from us. "Go, do what you have to do."

Joe headed off, hugging the wall. "I can probably us a leaf or something to clean myself!"

"Too much information Joe. Way more than I need to know!"

As Joe made his way to the corner, I stood face to face with this beetle. I gave the beetle a polite little wave. "Ah, hi Mr. or Mrs. Blue Beetle," I said softly.

The beetle stood there. I figured he was trying to figure out what I was.

"Believe me beetle, I'm just as confused as you are. Would you believe that when I woke up this morning I was a normal sized person? Yep, I would have looked at you and thought, cool little beetle. But now we're equal in size. Life is so weird. Don't you think?"

Yes, I was having a discussion about life with a beetle, while my best friend snuck off into a corner to poop. I hoped that I could delay the beetle from possibly eating me until my friend's poop lured the beetle away. Yeah, if this didn't teach me not to mess with my mom's inventions...then nothing would.

I smiled at the beetle. "Nice weather we're having? How about that Bobby kid? He and his sister Meg are certainly excitable. I wonder if they have too much sugar in their diet? Hard to believe they're related to Zac. Zac is so calm and dreamy! I wonder if they might be adopted? Or maybe Zac's adopted? Life is so complicated sometimes. Isn't it beetle?"

The beetle nudged a little closer to me. It flapped its wings. I jumped back. Mostly because I didn't know the beetle had wings.

I held up my hand. "Sorry, you kind of caught me off guard with that move." I gave the beetle a big smile. "I had no idea beetles had wings. What kind of music do you like?" I asked, even though I had no idea why I'd asked that.

The beetle wiggled its feelers or antennae, or whatever those sharp pointy things on its head were.

I gulped.

The beetle turned and headed away from me. He made a straight line to the corner. Joe came up to me with a big smile of relief on his face. "Wow, I feel so much lighter now!" he said. "It's amazing how it helps when you —"

"TMI Joe! TMI!" I shouted.

Joe nodded. "Right, got it. Too much information. Sorry."

He pointed to the beetle and smiled. "Looks like our plan worked!"

"I'll give you total credit for that plan, Joe. Feel free to call it your plan. Yes, your plan worked."

Joe looked at me with a wide grin. "Now what? Do we sit and wait for Bobby to come back?"

I considered our options. I didn't love the idea of being stuck in a bug house with a big beetle and Joe's poop. I also didn't love the idea of being at the mercy of a hyper five-year-old.

I started looking around for a way out of this aquarium tank. After all, it couldn't hold the ants, so no way it could hold a couple of smart kids like Joe and me. I pointed to the corner of the cage, there was a crack in the cover.

"That crack must have been how the ants got out!" I said. "If the ants managed to escape, so can we!"

Joe looked at the crack. He looked back at me. "Yeah but ants can stick to things and climb walls. Unless you're secretly Spiderman, neither of us can do that!"

Yes, Joe had a point. But I didn't love the idea of our fate being in the hands and mouth of Bobby.

Chapter 18

Looking around our new "home" I saw a big stick on top of the dirt. I wasn't sure why Bobby had dropped it in here. I guessed he had done it to give his pet ants something to climb along. It was hard to figure Bobby out...was he a nice little kid or was he a brat?

I pointed to the stick. "We can use that!" I said.

"Ah okay," Joe said.

I walked over and picked up the stick. It felt much heavier than I thought it should. Instead of lifting it I dragged it to the corner as Joe watched. I gave Joe a look. It was my 'get over here and help me' look.

Amazingly Joe understood. He rushed over to me, reached down and helped me lift the stick up. Together we positioned the stick at an angle that should make it pretty easy to climb up.

"Okay," Joe said slowly. "We climb up this stick and get out of this ant prison. Then what?" he asked. "We'll be on top of it instead of in it. Not sure we'll be that much better off."

"We'd be free!" I said. "We're so small and light now, I don't think the fall from the top of this thing would hurt us."

Joe rubbed his chin. "No maybe not. But we'd still be up on the table. And that's a much bigger drop. I know the rug is soft and cushy, but I still think that fall would either hurt or kill us."

I started inching up the stick. "I'll worry about that when we're out of here!" I told Joe.

Joe let out a little exasperated gasp, and then followed me up the branch. "I'm glad we're good climbers!" he said.

Shimmering up to the top of the branch, I reached up through the hole in the cover Bobby had put over us. I felt kind of insulted that Bobby must have thought Joe and I were dumber than his ants. After all, the ants had worked out a way to escape. I pulled myself up onto the top ledge of the aquarium. I had just enough room for my feet. I slid to the side so Joe could follow my lead.

After a minute or so, Joe joined me on the top. We looked down at the table. "Err, that's quite a drop," Joe gulped. "You sure you want to do this?" he asked.

I looked down. "No, not really, but I don't want to be stuck in a tank with a bug."

"Well now we're stuck on top of it," Joe said.

"Agreed, but this is better. This is our choice, not the choice of some crazy five-year-old."

"Uh oh," Joe gulped. "Better be quiet about the crazy five-year-old."

"Why?" I took a moment to realize. "He's back. Isn't he?"

Joe nodded.

Bobby came rushing towards us. "Why are you out of your new home? Why do you think I'm crazy?" he asked.

Five-year-olds have good hearing.

I turned to Bobby. "We needed fresh air! That home is kind of stinky," I told him.

Bobby leaned over and took a whiff of the aquarium. "Wow it smells like poop!"

Joe turned red.

Bobby looked at us. "But why did you call me

crazy?"

"Crazy means really cool in fairy talk!" I told him in my most serious voice. "It means the coolest of the cool. Crazy cool!"

"Exactly," Joe said. "And I have no idea why that place smells like poop."

Bobby shrugged, "I don't mind. I kind of like how poop smells, especially mine."

All right, time to change the subject from poop. "So, crazy cool Bobby where is your brother Zac?"

Bobby stomped on the floor. "Mom and my sister are out shopping and he's supposed to be watching me, but he's on the phone with some girl!"

"Oh, who?"

"Why does that matter?" Joe asked.

I shot Joe an annoyed look. He sank back a bit.

Bobby put his head over me, giving me a great view of his nostrils. "If you're a fairy, you should know who he's talking to."

"Of course I know. I'm just testing you!" I said.

Bobby grinned and shook his head. He crossed his arms. "You tell me!"

I had to admit, Bobby was sharper than I'd given him credit for. Still, there was no way I would lose this battle of wits. I knew the school. I knew Zac. I figured it had to be one of the two prettiest girls in our grade. It was either Ella Pane or Reanna Cole. Ella had shining dark hair and huge brown eyes. It seemed as though half the boys in my class liked her, a lot! Reanna had long wavy brown hair that curled around her face and onto her shoulders. Her eyes were an emerald shade of green, and everyone always commented on how pretty she was.

Both Ella and Reanna often hung out with Zac and

his friends. I'd seen them on numerous occasions chatting and laughing together. So I had a fifty-fifty shot here. I really didn't like either of those girls. They both seemed to think they were better than everyone else...just because they were popular. I actually had to admit that Ella was kind of nice. She always said hi to me. But still, she's not nearly good enough for Zac. Whereas Reanna never said a word to me. In fact, when she looked towards me she seemed to look through me. I'm pretty sure Reanna Cole didn't even realize I existed in the world. And with my luck, it had to be her.

"Her name is Reanna!" I said firmly.

Bobby jumped up and down clapping. "You are magic!"

"More like really nosy," Joe said under his breath.

I ignored Joe. I pointed to Bobby. "See, I have great magic. Now please take me to your brother!"

Bobby leaned into me. "If you're so magical, why do you want to see my brother?"

"He has a good point there," Joe told me, loud enough for Bobby to hear.

"Not helping here, Joe!" I quietly scolded.

"See, your servant thinks I know stuff!" Bobby told me.

Time to think this out. As strange as it was, I needed to convince Bobby to take me to see Zac now. How funny that I went from being horrified that Zac would see me like this...to Zac being my big hope. Of course, if I were going to see Zac soon I would need to get through to Bobby. How hard could it be to trick a hyper little kid?

"Look Bobby, I know that you like to play games, right?"

Bobby smiled. "I do!"

"Do you know how to play rock, paper, scissors?" I asked.

Bobby snickered. "Of course, I'm not stupid! I beat my mommy at it all the time!"

I looked at Bobby with my eyes wide open and my jaw dropped, pretending to be impressed. "Well, then you are very very good!" I said.

"Yep! The best!" Bobby boasted, chest out.

I pointed to myself and then back to him. "I will beat you at rock, paper, scissors to show you how I am so magical."

"You got it!" Bobby shouted.

He curled his hand into a ball. I curled my hand into a ball. Time to use my brain here. Bobby certainly wasn't a paper kind of guy. No way. I doubted he was a scissors fan either. Nope, Bobby was a rock. He had that rock kind of mind that just wanted to smash things.

To help my point I said, "I bet you really rock at this!"

"I do!" Bobby squealed.

"On three!" I said.

"One!" we swung our arms.

"Two!" we swung our arms the other way.

"Three!" I shouted. I put my hand in the middle and opened it up for paper.

Sure enough Bobby left his fist closed in the rock form.

His face dropped as I covered his rock hand with my paper hand and said, "Paper covers rock!"

Bobby let out a giant sigh. Once again blasting me with breath that smelled of old milk.

"I also know that you love milk!" I told him.

He looked at me. "Yep, it's my favorite. Zac, can't drink milk cause it makes him fart!" Bobby added.

"I knew that!" I said.

Joe leaned into me and whispered. "You do. Man you pay a lot of attention to this guy."

I turned to Joe. "Oh please! Like you don't obsess over girls! You know Ruby Parsons' schedule by heart. I've seen you hanging out by the door after class, just so you can see her!"

Joe stammered. "Well, well, ah she might drop something and need me to pick it up..."

Bobby put his hands on his hips and looked at us. "For magic fairies you guys fight a lot!"

I pointed at Bobby and locked my eyes on him. "Look Bobby, enough fooling around! Take us to your brother now, or I send a magic message to your mom telling her that your ants have escaped!"

Bobby gasped, "How did you know my mom doesn't know?"

Pointing to myself I said, "I've got the magic, remember!" I lifted my arms up angrily. "Now, take me to your brother, Zac! Or else!!"

Bobby leaned forward and reached for me.

"Careful!" I cautioned. "Squeeze too tight and I will fart in your hand!" I warned.

"Okay!" Bobby said, gently lifting me off the aquarium tank.

He turned to walk away.

Joe cleared this throat behind us. "Ahem!" he said loudly.

From Bobby's hand, I pointed at Joe. "My fairy servant magic Joe needs to come too!"

Bobby squinted at me. "Joe isn't a very magical

name! And you know he really hasn't done anything magic!"

I grinned. "He has done magic! You just haven't seen it. His magic is so powerful, if you saw it you would pee your pants!"

"Yes!" Joe said making a fist.

Bobby shook his head. "Oh, Mom doesn't like it when I pee my pants."

"Yeah, I can imagine nobody likes that!" Joe said loudly. "Plus you must not like it either!"

Bobby nodded. "Yeah, it makes my pants too squishy and smelly."

I'd had about enough of peeing the pants talk. "Just take him with us and all will be fine."

Bobby reached over and picked up Joe. "Can you make my brother, Zac pee his pants? Now that would be funny!"

"Oh, I agree!" Joe said.

"There will be no peeing in pants by anyone!" I said firmly.

Bobby moved Joe closer to his face. "Is she always so cranky and bossy?"

Joe smiled. "She can be fun at times. She just gets a little too serious occasionally. You know how girls can be!"

Bobby looked at him. "I can't figure out girls at all."

"Believe me kid, you're not alone!" Joe said.

I pointed to the door. "Can we get moving please!"

Bobby looked at me now. "You said please, but I don't think you sounded like you meant it."

"Please!" I said, batting my eyes.

Bobby walked out of his room. Finally, we were making progress. At last, I would get to see Zac, and he could help us out of this mess.

My mind started racing again. Are we doing the right thing? Is this really how I want Zac to see me? I mean come on, I'm two inches tall! What kind of impression is that going to make on Zac? Not only that, I look terrible! I mean my hair is a mess. I've been in the same clothing all day. I've been dropped in dirt. I've fought with ants, spiders and beetles. I've been next to poop. Man, I couldn't smell very good either. Plus, I would have to admit to Zac, the best looking boy in the school, that I had been dumb enough to shrink myself. Not only me, but also my best buddy, Joe. Oh no! What if Zac thought Joe was my boyfriend? I mean he is a boy and he is my friend, but he's not my boyfriend. But now Joe and I are on this adventure together so…

Joe looked over at me. "You're having second thoughts about letting Zac see you like this."

"Maybe," I admitted.

"Look, Bella, I get it. You're scared, but I really don't see another way out of this."

I exhaled and sighed. Joe was right. I had to let Zac see me like this so he could call for help. Hopefully we would grow closer over this. A funny story to tell our kids.

Bobby went downstairs. He carried us into the living room. No Zac to be found. "Zac! Zac!" he called.

"I'm busy right now!" Zac called. From the muffled sound of his voice, I could tell he had to be in another room.

Bobby looked at us. "He's gotta be in the bathroom. This could take a while! Unless you want to go in?"

"NO!" Joe and I both shouted.

Okay this may actually have been the first good break Joe and I had since we'd shrunk. "Bobby is there a phone in the house?"

"Of course, my mom and dad and Zac all have

108

phones! I will too, when I'm ten!"

"I mean, is there a house phone? A big one that everybody can use?" I asked.

"Yep, in the kitchen!" Bobby said.

"Take us to that one!" I said.

"Why?" Bobby asked.

"So I can call Fairyland and maybe get you a few more wishes!" I told him.

"Oh good!" Bobby gushed. He rushed into the kitchen. Sure enough there was a phone on the wall.

Bobby put us down on the table next to the phone. He took the phone off the hook. "You're too small to press the buttons so I'll do it for you!" he said showing surprising insight.

"Here's the deal Bobby. You dial the number and then put the phone down next to us and I'll do the talking."

"Right!" Bobby said. "What's the number?"

I said, "5"

Bobby pushed the five.

"5"

Bobby pushed the five again.

"5"

Bobby pushed the five again. He looked at me. "You can speak faster. I know my numbers, I'm not stupid!"

"Right! 8 5 4 0!" I said.

Bobby hit the numbers. He plopped the phone hand set down on the table. I could hear it ringing.

"Hello?" Becky said from the phone.

"Becky! It's me!" I shouted into the mouthpiece.

"Bella?" Becky replied. "Where are you? Mom says it's time for you to help me with my homework for tomorrow!"

"Becky, you have to give Mom a message for me!" I said.

"Why?" Becky asked.

"Becky, just tell mom that Joe and I had an accident with one of her inventions."

"What do you mean?" Becky asked.

"Becky, tell Mom we're trapped at 205 East North Street! It's Zac's house!"

"Why are you there?" Becky asked.

"Becky, there was an accident with Mom's

machine and we got shrunk. Now we need Mom to come get us and unshrink us!"

Becky laughed. "Ha! Serves you right!"

"Becky, please!"

The phone clicked.

Well the good news was, we got our message out. Becky now knew we were in trouble and where we were. The bad news was that we were helpless until Becky decided to tell Mom.

"She will tell your mom, right?" Joe asked.

"Yeah…" I said, I just had to hope she told Mom before we got squashed or Zac saw me like this.

The end for now!

Find out what happens next in
I Shrunk My Best Friend - Book 2
Zac to the Rescue!
Available NOW!!

Thanks so much for reading
I Shrunk My Best Friend!
Book 1

If you enjoyed it, could you please leave a review?
We can't wait to hear what you think!
Thanks heaps!
Katrina and John ☺

Here's some more funny books that we hope you enjoy...

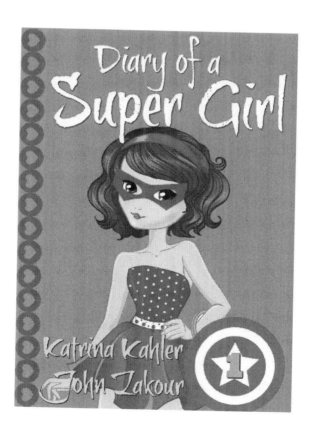

***

About the Authors

John Zakour *is a Humor/SF/Fantasy writer with a Master's Degree in Human Behavior. He has written thousands of gags for syndicated comics, comedians and TV Shows (including the Simpsons, Rugrats and Joan River's old TV show). John also writes a daily comic called Working Daze.*

Katrina Kahler *is the Best Sellling Author of several series of books, including Julia Jones' Diary, Mind Reader, The Secret, Diary of a Horse Mad Girl, Twins, Angel, Slave to a Vampire and numerous Learn to Read Books for young children.*
Katrina lives in beautiful Noosa on the Australian coastline.

Like us on Facebook http://bit.ly/FreeBooksForKidsFB

And follow us on Instagram

@juliajonesdiary

@freebooksforkids

Remember to subscribe to our website bestsellingbooksforkids.com so we can notify you as soon as we release a new book.

22168222R00066

Printed in Great Britain
by Amazon